My Last Forty Days

A Visionary Journey among the Pueblo Spirits

Felicitas D. Goodman

Illustrations by Susan Josephson

INDIANA UNIVERSITY PRESS

BLOOMINGTON & INDIANAPOLIS

The paper used in this publication meets the minimum requirements of
American National Standard for Information Sciences—Permanence of Paper
for Printed Library Materials, ANSI Z39.48-1984.

Manufactured in the United States of America

Library of Congress Cataloging-in-Publication Data

Goodman, Felicitas D.
My last forty days : a visionary journey
among the Pueblo spirits / Felicitas D. Goodman.
p.   cm.
Includes bibliographical references.
ISBN 0-253-33310-5 (cl : alk. paper).—
ISBN 0-253-21135-2 (pa : alk. paper)
1. Pueblo mythology—Fiction.   I. Title.
PS3557.05833M9   1997
813'.54—dc21   97-5108

1 2 3 4 5 02 01 00 99 98 97

My Last Forty Days

SUNRISE

They each took a last puff from their pipe,
and the smoke glowed pink and golden
over the horizon.
Then the Medicine Man pointed down:
"See that one with her long gray hair?
She's another one that got away."
They looked at each other,
narrow eyes squinting,
and had themselves a belly laugh,
two old men remembering their youth.
And while the Medicine Man settled on a cloud,
Father Sun started on his daily round.

CONTENTS

INTRODUCTION

The languages of dreaming, being highly imagistic and affective, are only with great difficulty translated into rational systems of interpretation and thought. The shaman's art is not the translation of dreams into verbal interpretation; rather it is the use of dreams, the praxis through which events are transformed or guided in accordance with dream or visionary experience.
—Lee Irwin

THE TALE you are about to read is a visionary adventure story. What gives it its visionary quality is first of all its special kind of protagonist: the narrator is a ghost. However, not all ghost stories are visionary. In fact, most are not, for they take place against the backdrop of everyday, ordinary reality, which is part of their allure. What makes this ghost story a visionary one is the fact that in addition the events take place not in the ordinary realm but in its companion world, popularly called the alternate reality.

We all know a great deal about the ordinary world, not only because we live in it but also because there are uncounted historical records and travelogues available that provide ample information about those of its regions that we are unfamiliar with. By contrast, the alternate reality is shrouded in mystery, although its historical record is equally available, contained in its myths. We run into difficulties when we try to locate some reliable travelogues. For although the two realities or realms share a number of characteristics—for instance, they consist of a large number of divergent regions, and they have many kinds of inhabitants representing vastly different lifestyles or cultures—ease of access is not one of them.

In order to travel to some out-of-the-way country of the ordinary realm, all we need is travel money and the right set of papers. Not so with the other realm. Money and a passport would be of no use at all if we wanted to cross its borders. In order to visit there, we need to change not our identity papers and our legal tender but our very way of seeing, the manner in which our body functions. Put differently, we have to alter our state of consciousness from the ordinary one, suitable for our life in the everyday reality, and change over to the one suitable for getting around in the alternate one. This special state is termed the ecstatic trance.[1] Experienced travelers in that realm, shamans and medicine people, are familiar with such border-crossing procedures, but at least in the past, not many were given to talking about the details of their adventures to the outsider upon returning. Consequently we are faced by a lamentable dearth of reliable travelogues dealing with the countries of that other realm. The reason is that it used to be downright dangerous to give even an oral report about a sojourn "over there," let alone one in writing. That was what got the witches of old into so much trouble.[2]

Here, for instance, is a story illustrating the point that historical research recently unearthed.[3]

It seems that in a snowy valley of the Alpine hinterland, on the third of February 1578, two shepherds of the village of Oberstdorf, Chonrad Stoeckhlin and his friend Jacob Walch, sat together enjoying a crock of wine. As the evening wore on, their conversation drifted to ultimate concerns, to death and dying. What might the great Beyond be like? No one seemed to know. So it occurred to them to make this pledge: whichever one of them died first would let the other one in on the secret. It was a solemn pact, and they shook hands on it. Unexpectedly, a mere eight days later, Jacob Walch died, and he did keep his promise. From the Beyond, he came back and taught Chonrad how to lie still, turned on his side, and to hearken to his voice. The simple strategy made it possible for Chonrad to join his friend Jacob Walch on the Other Side. Jacob's ghostly presence and the spirit helpers that he brought along guided Chonrad into a province of the alternate reality, familiar and yet strange, populated by gnomes, giants, and fairies, by Good Women who helped people and healed the sick, and by multitudes of the spirits of the dead. He provided a spirit guide for Chonrad, a special angel who took him along to joyous revelries with song and dance and sumptuous meals, who taught him how to fly and how to heal and to divine. Foolishly, Chonrad did not keep his newfound knowledge to himself. And so eventually, as was bound to happen in a world ruled by the Inquisition, he and twenty of his fellow villagers, men and women who had listened to him, were horribly tortured and burned at the stake.

The question is, of course, why Chonrad was not supposed to enter that magical realm in the first place. That all goes back to the story of Adam and Eve. As is well known, this couple was at one time living in a magical place called Eden, as a certain province of the alternate reality was called at that time. It was a pretty enough place; there were lots of flowers, many trees, a gaily chattering brook, and friendly animal people. Foremost among the latter was a wise snake, which Eve loved to spend time with rather than with Adam, who was not very bright. As Eve mentioned to Snake Woman, she put up with him because he was the only man around. Besides, gossip had it that he kept another woman hidden somewhere in the back bushes, but then perhaps the animal people were just talking to pass the time. More likely he was hanging out with one of the male spirits, the one who titled himself "god" and tried to order everyone around all the time, even telling the animal people what to do, such as: you lions are not supposed to eat rabbits; that's beastly; far better you ate grass. Needless to say, the lions were not listening.

Meanwhile, Eve and the snake were having a good time playing around with the plants. Maybe this jasmine would be prettier here, not over there by the rock? So let's transplant it. And how about this little fruit tree? If we moved it to this sunny spot, it would probably grow faster, and have larger apples. That was the way they went about enjoying themselves.

One day, as the two of them passed the spot where they had planted the tree, Eve noticed that not only had it grown taller, but it also had much larger apples than before. She picked one, and as Adam was just sauntering by, she generously let him have it. At that very moment, to her utter amazement, that domineering spirit that Adam was chummy with appeared next to the tree completely out of nowhere. Unaccountably, he flew into a frightful rage. They had not asked him if they could transplant that tree! And who gave them permission to eat those apples? He was furious, shouting very loudly and really having a temper tantrum. Eden was his place, he kept repeating, and if they did not follow his orders, they had no business in Eden any longer. Then he grabbed both of them by their hair and threw them out the gate. And to top it all off, with his magic he made a fiery rotating sword appear on the outside of the big door, so that they would not be able to come back in.

As could be expected, Adam blamed Eve forever after for spoiling the good life for him, and they never did make it back into Eden again, not in their lifetime and not even after death.

As Adam and Eve had found out, that spirit who had made himself ruler of Eden was extremely vindictive. Actually, of course, Eden had never been the only province of the alternate reality. But to make people as miserable as possible—sinners, he called them—that was what he wanted them to believe, and he had his priests swear that they would never divulge the existence of other magical regions to any human. And so he had the priests adopt the rule that whosoever would maintain that there were other countries in the alternate realm in addition to Eden, some even more gorgeous than his garden, let alone possibly even visit there, was to be put to death. So that was what happened to hapless Chonrad. Since he insisted that he had been "out there," they maintained that because it could not have been Eden, it must have been the Bad Place. By a strange quirk of logic, that made him evil, too, and so of course he had to be killed.

Much has happened since Chonrad Stoeckhlin's fiery death. The priests and their allies went about conquering the earth, and eventually they could no longer execute everyone who had been to various provinces of the alternate reality other than Eden. There were just too many of them. So they mounted a powerful ad campaign to convince the general public that the alternate reality did not really exist, that it was all so much superstition and childish fancy. It should all be forgotten.

Luckily, not everyone fell for that line, or we should all

have become frightfully poor, with an important part of our reality declared nonexistent. Instead, around the world, people paid no attention to the advertisements and continued learning how to visit their respective provinces of the alternate reality, often at great risk to themselves. Some were even bold enough to tell about it. In this country, for instance, much of this secret knowledge was actually written down.[4] So for those adventurous travelers anxious to read about it all, there are now indeed sufficient travelogues available to learn from.

What we understand from these various accounts is that in the same manner as the provinces of earth, the various sections of the alternate reality agree in some aspects. The power of gravity does not exist; neither does the tyranny of time prevail. People can fly and can visit faraway places and events and scenes of the long ago. And they can consort with the spirit beings that happen to be at home there. There is also information available now about the manner in which the borders can be crossed, that is, how the changes of the body are brought about that are necessary to that purpose. Some people dance to that purpose, others play drums or recite long mythic stories; the Plains Indians, spontaneously or during their vision quests, endure great hardship, hunger, thirst, and sometimes pain. Or people assume special ancient body postures, while a helper rattles for them, as we can see in the thousand-year-old rock painting. (See also Felicitas D. Goodman, 1990.) Or a person might enter upon death, as in the present visionary tale. What people encounter upon arriving, however, is enormously different. A Siberian shaman might climb the Tree of the World and encounter the Iron Bird in a nest, sitting on a mysterious egg in which the soul of a young shaman is growing. A medicine woman of the Plains has an encounter with the Ant People, who give her a healing medicine as a present. And a person assuming a special South American shape-shifting posture might turn into a jaguar. And the ghost of the lonely woman, the narrator of our story, long ago expelled from her homeland, enters the Pueblo Indian Province as an asylum seeker. What happens to her there is the topic of this visionary tale.

NOTES

1. For details, see Felicitas D. Goodman, *Where the Spirits Ride the Wind: Trance Journeys and Other Ecstatic Experiences* (Bloomington: Indiana University Press, 1990).

2. Carlo Ginzburg, *Hexensabbat* (Berlin: Wagenbach, 1990).

3. Wolfgang Behringer, *Chonrad Stoeckhlin und die Nachtschar: Eine Gschichte aus der fruehen Neuzeit* (Munich: Piper, 1994).

4. Lee Irwin, *The Dream Seekers: Native American Visionary Traditions of the Great Plains* (Norman: University of Oklahoma Press, 1994).

My Last Forty Days

I should have known that after I died things would be different than I had imagined. During my morning prayer I had so often said it to my Friend, my older brother, the mighty Invisible One, that it seemed like it could be no other way: "And when I step across that line for the last time, I know you'll be there and take me to the Lake." But of course he was not there.

To be honest, I had had my doubts whether things would truly go all that smoothly. Who knows whether I would even be admitted? Would the Wood Spirits, guardians of the entrance to the Lake, recognize me and take me below? I was not born a Tewa Indian; no one had performed the requisite rituals over me, the naming, the giving of the water, the rest. I had received a Tewa name, Povi, meaning flower, but it was not awarded to me when I was a babe, during that sacred occasion when the women presented the newborn to the sun. Rather, a well-meaning elderly Indian lady had hunted it out for me in a printed Tewa Indian list of names. It was such a mundane occasion, it seemed so phony that I never claimed that name as my own. So I supposed it probably did not count. Of course I was hoping that my yearning, my searching, my research and my teaching, my daily offerings of blue cornmeal would make up for my illegitimacy. And had not a famous cacique once proposed marriage to me? Of course it was long ago and in jest, I knew that, but still I had hoped that it might carry some weight, even if only a little bit. But apparently it did not.

I was standing on the ridge on my last morning, as I had every morning, waiting for the sun to rise and burst upon the world with its jeweled light. Behind me New Mexico's Jemez Mountains, hiding under their dark mantle the secret they witnessed eons ago as humans struggled up through the rocks from the dank and dark Third World into the sunny, verdant Fourth one. I filled my lungs with the pure dry air of fall that they too must have breathed on that first day, the Corn Mothers, the Hunter-Healer, the Corn Maidens, the men and the women, and the children. In front of me the peak which they called the Mountain of the Stone Man, with its double hump, and the mountains to the right of it, one of them pitifully scarred by the gashes of the Ski Basin. That hurt. So I turned around and glanced for consolation down into the valley and the immense, sprawling dry riverbed. How majestic it must have been when it still carried water, home to uncounted water beings, fish, frogs, mosquitoes, before hundreds of years ago the great droughts choked life out of it. Now it was a river of sand.

I turned to the weather-worn old juniper next to me. It

stretched its gnarled skinny branches to the sky, old like my hands, knobby and wrinkled. I was going to start the blessing, greeting the Spirits, as I had done for years on end every morning, every evening, when it happened, at the very moment when the sky blushed and then fleetingly paled as Father Sun's first rays streaked over the peaks and the golden cloud fleeces. My clothes disappeared and along my uplifted hands, my arms, my face, my trunk, my thighs, the skin split open as though the morning breeze had pulled a zipper. Limply, my worn-out body cloak crumpled down to the russet-colored sand, transparent like the discarded skin of a rattlesnake, and spread out over the small stone ring in which we had so often burned copal to please the Spirits. A startled tip beetle, called disrespectfully a stinkbug by the locals, clambered out from under my left elbow skin and looked around, its antennae trembling in obvious disgust. It lifted its back end to spray, and finding no one to attack, hurried away, its six skinny legs flying, toward an unknown destination.

I looked around, startled. So this was it. I had stepped across the line. I had died. Yet everything was as it had been before, the sky, the mountains, the earth, the juniper, only its quality was different, as though saturated with light and almost imperceptibly vibrating. I looked down on myself. I had some of that same quality, transparent, yet of substance. But where was my Friend? I really had been convinced that we had that agreement. Without him to guide me to the Lake, where was I to go? Would I just sit here and disintegrate? It was obvious that I could not turn to the ordinary world for help, having no visible body any more. My friends, my children, my grandchildren would no longer be able to see me. They would mournfully gather up my discarded cloak, perhaps even think it was me, then have it cremated and bury it as I had directed, all the while not even realizing that I was still around. I was beginning to feel utterly, totally disconsolate.

The air was still. The ever-present noise of the rush of traffic on the highway in the valley below was hushed. Only a solitary little flycatcher chirped in the pinyon by the road, and four ravens flew in formation toward the pink cliffs on the northern horizon. Suddenly, the sound of a tiny bell broke the silence. A rush of joy washed over me. Of the many Spirit Beings living around here, Cricket was the first one that had befriended me so long ago. "Cricket Spirit," I called out, "hey, little sister, where are you?" "Turn around and look down," a small voice said, and then there was more ringing of the silver bell. I looked down, but all I could see was the tiniest little fleck of twinkling light, smaller than that of a glow worm, in among the twisted juniper roots. "I am not sure I found you," I complained. "Couldn't you maybe jump up to a branch?" There was silence, and I was worried that perhaps I had scared my tiny sister away. Instead, I now heard the tintinnabulation almost at my feet, and then the thin, silvery voice suggested that I might want to sit down. Which I did.

The speck of light settled on my knee, which I noticed appeared soft and young, as did the rest of my translucent body. Of course, it no longer mattered, but it still was nice.

"I heard you next to my room last night," I said, just to start the conversation going. The spot flickered.

"I like to keep tabs on you. That is why I was here this morning. You seem sad. Want to talk of old times?"

It was tempting. There were these happy memories. Like when Cricket lured me to the forgotten shrine here on the land, or when in Yucatan she kept me awake with her silver voice during a most distressingly boring sermon that I was supposed to record.

As if guessing my thoughts, the little light said, "You

almost fell off the chair that time, you were so sleepy." The
tiny voice faded into a merry chime.

"And in the end, you got hoarse; I thought that was
so touching," I said. "You know, I often wondered, do all
crickets have human charges?"

"Oh no. Most crickets are just crickets, although they all
possess a diminutive spark connecting them to the Spirit
world. I am different, one of the First People. Like maybe
a cricket prototype. You know what they say: if a cricket
looks like a cricket and acts like a cricket, it probably is
a cricket. But if it looks like a cricket but does not act like
a cricket, then most likely it is something else. Watch."

Actually, I had heard that said about birds. But no matter: the minute speck of light seemed to twist, a black tail
appeared, a pair of legs, then another pair, then in the most
comical way the third pair of legs pulled what looked like
a black hood from the back over the hunched front, and a
shiny black cricket complete with sculpted body and long
antennae was sitting on my knee. Then it shuddered and it
was a dot of light once more.

"Hey, that's neat," I exclaimed. "Could I do that too?"

"I am afraid not," it said. "You lost your human garment, and that is it. You can't put it back on. You are
now—" there was a bit of hesitation, "actually, you are
now, technically speaking, a ghost."

I knew that my Cricket sister was right, but it took a bit
of getting used to. So I changed the subject.

"Do you have any idea where my Friend is, my older
brother? I thought we were going to meet here, and that he
was going to take me to the Lake."

"Why do you want to go to the Lake?"

"Doesn't everyone get to go there eventually? I mean the
privileged ones, those with the right credentials. At least
that's what tradition says. And then they just sit around

with all their friends and relatives; there is song and laughter all the time, and they watch the Kachinas dance forever. It must be wonderful." I heaved a heavy sigh. "If my Friend doesn't show up, can you take me?"

"I am afraid I can't help you there. I do not go to the Lake. I stay around here and ring my bell. Those are the rules."

I wanted to ask if she thought that I could find my way there alone, when there was a noise on the road leading up to the ridge. Someone was coming. I got up and peeked through the pinyon branches. Huffing and puffing, a most curious fellow was making his way over the ruts and stones. He was actually a squash. Or to put it more exactly, he was two squashes, a smaller one for his head and the larger one for his body. He was wearing a short black apron with green and red embroidery; he was carrying a cane, and he was clearly looking for someone, peering this way and that way over the hills to the east and to the west.

I stepped out from behind the pinyon to have a clearer look.

"Ha," he said in a deep and raspy voice, "so there you are. We surmised this would be the day."

I was bewildered. That was not at all what I thought my Friend would look like. No brown fur, no pointed horns, nothing like what I had seen in my visions.

"Are you my Friend?" I asked.

He shook his squash head. "I think I know what you mean, although you are not being very precise. I am the Messenger, and I am surprised that you do not recognize me. And I have a message from your Friend."

"Do sit down and rest," I said, trying not to show how disappointed I was.

"I can't do that. I have other messages to carry. Like prayers for rain to the Cloud People, although right now this is my off-season. But you are not the only one who is expecting information, you know."

"No, I really didn't know that. I thought all you Spirit Beings were omniscient."

He shook his head and there was a tone of exasperation in his voice.

"No, no, my dear," he said, "there are no omnis around here. Nobody is omniscient, or omnipotent, or whatever other omni. So of course you need messengers." I thought I had better wait until he said what he had to say. Ceremoniously, he wiped his squash forehead with a red kerchief. Then he said, quite civilly, "Your Friend is sorry, but he cannot come today. He is unavoidably detained."

I was feeling irritated. Why do messengers always have to be so pompous? "So what's keeping him? After all, I need to get to the Lake!"

"Oh, haven't you heard? A white buffalo calf was born far east of here, in a part of the country that you white people call Wisconsin. It is a momentous occasion, of great social and religious import, and your Friend is directing some of the rituals the Spirits are organizing to welcome it."

I felt chastened. I could see where the death of an old white woman like me could not hold a candle to the birth of a sacred white buffalo calf. "I am sorry," I apologized. "I didn't have any idea. But do you think that he will perhaps come tomorrow? I am in a hurry, you know. I need to get to the Lake."

The squash man turned to go, and over his shoulder, he said, "Maybe he will. But really, I wouldn't worry. After all, you have forty days to get there." And he hurried off toward the gate.

"Thank you," I called after him, and turning to Cricket, who had settled in a juniper branch, I asked, "What did he mean, I have forty days? I thought it took only four?"

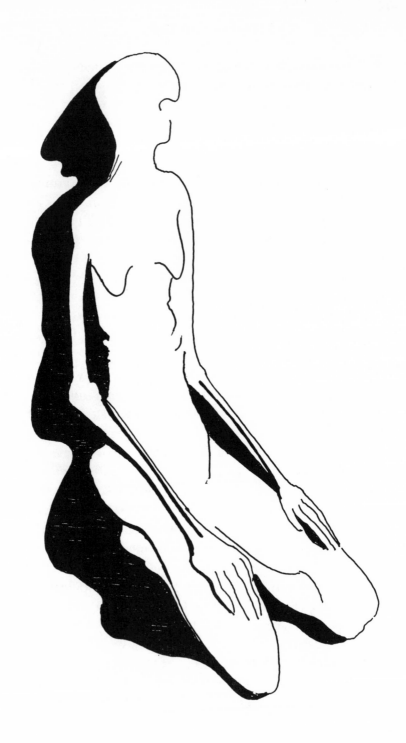

"You are different. It will take you that long to change from a ghost into a spirit," she explained casually. "Ghosts are not admitted to the Lake."

Dejectedly, I sat down on the ground once more. "So what can I do now?"

"Why don't you play for a while? We all do a lot of that around here. Maybe do some shapeshifting. You used to be good at that."

It seemed a workable idea. I knelt down and placed my hands on my thighs. Then it struck me: I had no rattle and no one to rattle for me. Without that, I could not do any shapeshifting. I was still pondering the problem when I heard a small voice whisper into my ear: "Call your rattle!"

"Was that you, Cricket?" I asked. But Cricket had jumped off to the next juniper, trilling away. So I did as I was told. "Sound good, little sister," I said, as I used to when I was still a human, "sound sweet." And instantly, in front of me there was my rattle, sounding away, eagerly dancing, its handle rocking back and forth like a pendulum. So I closed my eyes. Actually, I thought, I probably didn't need to do that. After all, I was in the alternate reality already. But I did it anyway.

A whirlwind grasped me and tore me apart, until all my ghostly particles danced with it, round and round. I was nothing but dust in the wind. It laughed and dropped me, and I settled on the ground, and when I looked, I was a skeleton. I wanted to scream, but now I, the skeleton, grew claws, and legs, a tawny sinewy body, and a tail. I knew that I had a cat's face and small ears, and that I was a mountain lion. I scampered down the side of the hill, scattering pebbles, and started running in the riverbed. What joy to be bounding along so light and free! A cottontail jumped out of a clump of mountain mahogany and I went in pursuit, my saliva dripping in anticipation of the kill. But then it was I who was the rabbit racing along the narrowing avenues of the old river. I loved that too, but it did not last. I turned into a dragonfly on sparkling wings, felt tired, and to rest, I settled on a shimmering round boulder. I was feeling very hot, ever hotter. And just when I thought I could not bear it any longer, my body split open, and I gave birth to a ball of light that rolled down into the sand.

I opened my eyes and was on the ridge once more. Cricket was settled on our copal altar, and my old human body garment was gone.

"What happened?" I asked.

"Your children and friends collected your discarded cloak while you were away. They were very sad."

"I must go to them, tell them that I am here and that I am all right."

"You can't do that."

"Why not?"

"The contact with ghosts makes the living very ill. You must stay away from them."

Another one of those rules. I had still been kneeling, so now I sat more comfortably on the sand and embraced my legs. "Maybe I'll go to my room and rest." I said.

There was a tone of real regret in Cricket's voice. "I am sorry, but that is also against the rules. In fact, your friends will have to change the appearance of your room, so you won't even be able to find it."

"Why in the world would they do that?"

"It's for your own good, really. If you keep going back to your human home, you'll never turn into a spirit. You'll stay a ghost instead, and believe me, that is not very pleasant."

I could see the point. Besides, ghosts were not allowed under the Lake. So I would certainly not want to stay one forever and ever. I sighed. All these regulations were really difficult to get used to.

"Then where can I rest?" There was a small titter. "You need no rest, silly. Ghosts never sleep. Besides, they like to be about in the night."

"Maybe so. Still, it would make things easier if I could pretend that I go to sleep at night. Of course, for that I would need to have my own home. But getting that is probably impossible before I go to the Lake."

"Actually, you already have one. Look over there."

I turned west and looked at the rolling hills beyond the old riverbed. Secreted in one of the folds there was a curious formation. It looked from this vast distance like an old, very small adobe house nestled in among some junipers, its side walls and roof growing out of the rocks behind it. I had called it a spirit house when I first set eyes on it, for it kept disappearing and I could see it only when the shadows were just right shortly before sunset.

"Remember when you saw that for the first time? How sad you were because one of your friends had been rude to you, like out of the blue?"

"It was his medication; he couldn't help it."

"You were very sad nonetheless. So your Friend made it appear to you, to make you glad. Let's go see it."

I was afraid that it would be a strenuous, long hike, and I was not sure that I was up to that. "Stretch out your arms," that mysterious voice that I had heard before whispered into my ear. So I did. A strong air current grabbed hold of me. I just had time to settle Cricket on my shoulder, and off we went, across the riverbed and up into the hills, and in a wink landed in front of the Spirit House.

I looked it over. It was very ancient indeed. Its foundation consisted of loosely piled rocks like you find in the arroyos, those deep gashes that furrow the desert all over around here. The walls were not built of adobe bricks. Instead, they were puddled, like some of the ancestors used to do long before the white man came conquering. There was a small window, but what I had taken for a door from the distance was only a low juniper bush. Rather, for access, a rough wooden ladder with an ornately carved crossbar was leaning against the wall. A bunch of bright yellow marigolds grew out of a crack in the earth next to the right corner.

"Look, Cricket, flowers! How beautiful!" I stepped over to admire them more closely, but softly like a breeze of fall they sang a little ditty:

> Spirit shadows of the flowers,
> Do not touch, do not touch,
> Do not tear.
> Spirit flower shadows,
> Yellow spirit shadows.

"I wasn't going to hurt them," I said defensively to Cricket.

"Aren't you going to look inside?" she asked.

I climbed up the ladder. There was a square hole in the roof; it was open, and another ladder led down to a single rectangular room with a brown skin, bald in spots, on the earthen floor and a fireplace in the far corner. "Ask Ash Boy for some fire," the voice whispered in my ear.

That seemed a sensible suggestion. Ash Boy and I were

friends from way back. When I was still a human, I once entered my room after a trance session with some of my students, and I felt a presence. It was like a cloud, but more delicate, as though consisting only of a faint outline, yet radiating power. I was afraid to move for fear I would disturb it, and it began retreating slowly toward my fireplace. I remembered reading about a kindly Tewa house spirit who made its home in the fireplace. From then on I now and then scattered a pinch of cornmeal into the fireplace as a greeting so it would not feel lonely.

"Ash Boy," I said as my whispering voice had directed, "please let me have a fire."

Instantly a red and orange flame rose from among the stones, as a flower would in the desert after a rain. That certainly was a welcome sight.

"Thank you, Ash Boy," I said, and sat down. Briefly, I thought I saw the shadow of a hooded Kachina face behind the flames.

"So you know Ash Boy?" Cricket asked, who was hiding, cricket fashion, in the hairs of the skin.

"Of course. There are all those stories about him and his twin brother hunting rabbits. Maybe that was why he came to our place. We had lots of cottontails at the time. And the witch woman, Grandmother Teeth, was trying to eat them."

And then we continued together, as though we had done it for years:

> Grandmother Spider hid them, she did,
> She hid them in a niche, she did,
> And when Grandmother Teeth reached for them,
> She turned her into a deer,
> Into a deer, she did,
> Into a deer.

And we laughed. "How come you know the story too?" I asked.

"I heard the Old People tell it during story time, in the cold of winter, when the snakes go hiding underground to sleep."

I sat down more comfortably. "Tell me," I asked, "what is that whispering voice I sometimes hear in my ear when I face a vexing problem, like a little while ago, when I didn't know how to cross the river, and just now about how to make a fire?"

"Oh that? That is Holy Wind." Apparently I was supposed to know all about it, but when I shook my head, Cricket continued. "Don't you remember? Holy Wind, which unbeknown to Father Sun advised the Hero Twins, sons of Changing Woman and the Woman of the White Shells, how to avoid being killed by their suspicious father?" Cricket was wont to say—don't you remember? Actually, I liked that. I apparently had been allowed to bring along what amounted to a treasure-trove of memory fragments to this new life and still had access to it at will.

"But it lived in Navajo country."

"So what? There are no boundaries for the Wind. Don't you remember how small whirlwinds kept dancing down your road?"

"I do remember. I used to get upset when the locals called them dust devils. I was convinced they were kindly spirits that were twirling the dust around and not devils. So that was Holy Wind?" Obviously, in addition to remembering, I also had a lot of new information to learn.

For a while, we watched the fire, Cricket chiming a little, then falling silent again.

"What we now need is supper," I said, and meant it as a joke.

Cricket did not answer. The dancing flames formed a

glowing cave, and I recalled how as a child, crouching in front of the tiled stove, I had seen, through the small mica window of the door, miniature dwarfs with pointed red caps frolicking in and out of the embers. I barely turned when there was a scraping on the ladder, thinking it was Cricket. But then somebody was clearing his throat. It was the Messenger instead.

"You have come?" I asked, Pueblo fashion.

"Yes."

"Sit down," I said. Unceremoniously, the Messenger settled down next to me on the skin. That was difficult to accomplish for someone who had only a squash for a body, but he managed. I tried to remember what the next polite thing to say used to be, for I wanted him to feel at home.

"It is not customary for a stranger," I recited, "to visit the house of a stranger without saying something of what may be in his thoughts."

"You learned that well," he nodded. "Like in the old days. I was on my way home, but the Breasts of the Earth, what you call the San Francisco Peaks, are still a way off, so I thought I'd check on how you are doing."

"Trying to learn all the new rules," I sighed.

There was a faint little noise on the ladder, and we both turned to see Cricket sliding down, a tiny light with an even tinier bag of light on its back. It passed between us and deposited its load on the skin. As we watched, the bag expanded; it turned into an earth-colored clay pot with a black design of kiva steps on one side and lightning on the other, and filled to the brim with blue cornmeal mush.

"Supper!" I exclaimed.

"You taught your friends well," Cricket said. "They provided the cornmeal when they said good night to Father Sun as he sank down behind the Jemez Mountains."

We fell to it and ate and ate. It was surpassingly delicious.

Amazing how far the essence of a pinch of blue cornmeal went when offered ceremonially in the alternate reality.

I invited the Messenger to stay the night; but he declined, and, clambering up the ladder, he vanished into the night.

"Let's go play," Cricket suggested. And that was exactly what we did. It was the night of the autumnal equinox. All was festive and bright with moonlight as we slipped in and out between the pinyons and the junipers, circled around glowing snake-grass bushes and chased noisy grasshoppers into the rabbit brush. Brother Porcupine sat on a branch, resting after his evening repast, but he was grumpy. He was probably still embarrassed that once, doing the posture of Calling the Game, we had teased him out of hiding when I was still a human.

"I don't think so," said Cricket, "he is always morose like that."

We surprised Sister Rattlesnake as she slithered down an incline, but she did not trust us, and with astounding speed she wriggled into a narrow hole. Brother Badger, brown and flat, lifted his nose as he caught sight of us, then shook himself and was a glob of vibrating light. The constant shapeshifting that everyone engaged in around here took some time getting used to. We also strayed into the Arroyo of the Owls; and, on silent wings, one of the huge birds streaked past us, then called from afar, hoooo, hoo, hoo. When I turned to look, it was a Spirit Person, decked out in festive Pueblo attire, embroidered shirt, scarf around his head, hurrying toward the highway in the direction of the Pueblos.

"Someone is ill, maybe," nodded Cricket.

I was getting weary. "I think I'll go home and pretend to rest," I announced as the moon was beginning to slip toward the horizon.

Ghosts don't sleep, Cricket had said, but perhaps I was still so close to having been a human that I dozed off anyway on my skin in front of the fireplace. For suddenly I opened my eyes and the faint light of early morning made the ladder cast a shadow. But there was also something else, as if the entire ancient riverbed, the slopes of the hills, and even my Spirit House were vibrating much more than before, as when a tuning fork is suddenly hit really hard.

Climbing up the ladder, I poked my head through the hatch hole and looked out. What I saw was a hulking dark shadow that seemed to fill half the width of the riverbed, and it was radiating a power such as I had never experienced before. Rapture, I thought; this was rapture. It made me vibrate, along with the little house, the junipers, and the clouds above in the pale morning sky.

"Come down, my dear," a pleasant and altogether ordinary male voice said. The huge shadow was gone, and by the marigolds on the corner there stood a middle-aged Indian man, dark face, in simple Plains Indian attire, fringed pants and jacket, a single eagle feather in his long black hair and a blanket draped around his shoulders.

"So here you are," he said. "Welcome, welcome." I was almost struck speechless as I clambered down and joined him.

"Your face," I gulped; "I have seen your face before! I thought I would die, that morning when I saw your face on my buffalo mask. That was what I knew from tradition: if you see a Spirit, you will die, burn to death, whatever. But I didn't. So I thought I had been mistaken."

He spread out his blanket and we sat down. "You were

right," he said, "it was my face. But by that time I thought you were strong enough, after all the experience you had gained coming to call on our side of reality. And you were."

"I used to talk to you so much. Every morning, every evening. And I wondered whether you could even hear me."

"That is hard for us. More like a whisper of the wind in the trees. Unless of course you came to our side of reality, as you so often did. But we do hear the intention when the address is respectful. And we try to answer."

"Like when I'd be saying the morning blessing, and there was no wind at all, and yet a single small branch would be moving?"

"Right."

"I often wondered what I should call you, my older brother. Was simply 'Buffalo' all right? You helped me find your image in among the rocks, so I knew the nature of the Spirit that had befriended me."

"That is who I am. But I never could understand your name."

"One of my given names translates as Seed Bearer."

"Seed Bearer Woman," he repeated slowly. "It is good. It will do until you decide on a different one. Maybe when you turn into a spirit." It seemed to be an opening for asking about the Lake, but then I felt shy about it.

"During our Masked Dance," I said instead, "I often turned into a buffalo."

"I saw that, and it gave me joy. I also saw how you wept when you caught sight of the shadow of your horns."

"I was sad because I remembered the vast herds that once roamed this land. And I also sometimes hated their exterminators with the fury of impotent rage." I thought I would be censured, but he said nothing.

For a while we sat there in total peace. A branch on the

juniper some way down the slope moved slightly, and I thought I saw the outline of a wolf.

"You know him?" asked Buffalo. I shook my head. He took a small beaded bag from his belt.

"Let us go into your house. I have some gifts for you."

Ash Boy had lit a fire, and when Buffalo opened the small bag and shook it, an ample, pliant yellow buffalo hide started spreading out on the floor and turned dark fur up. I knelt down on it, stroking it and enjoying its softness. He sat down next to me.

"Thank you," I said. "But I have nothing to give you in return."

"You gave me sustenance every morning and every evening for many years. And how about the special celebration at the full of the moon? Now it is my turn. That was the first thing we noted about you. Your gifts. And your compassion."

I had to laugh. "How I fumbled around. I felt so sorry for all you Spirits on this land. For centuries, I reasoned, after the Pueblo people fled from the Spanish, no one had brought you any food offerings. I thought of water first. I almost heard you laugh about that. Then I picked flowers. I knew that was not it either."

"Then you asked the cacique's daughter, and she told you. That was good. Or we might still be on a diet of water and decapitated flowers." He laughed good-naturedly and reached for his belt. "There is one other thing." He pulled out a colorful medicine bag and placed it on the skin. It had a double rainbow beaded on it and a purple flower with one leaf. He got up, and there was now a flat drum in his hand. Hitting it very softly, he started singing.

Heya, heya, heya, ho.
Seed Bearer Woman

On the buffalo rug,
Heya, heya, heya, ho.
She waits.

I rocked on my knees to the rhythm of his drum. There was singing: "Weye hene yahe yo," the strands of the entrance song to the buffalo dance. Two youths in buffalo costume, little feathers waving from the tips of their blackened horns, and a girl in an embroidered white manta were dancing on the skin, shaking their rattles. Fast they stepped, then slowly.

Buffalo stopped drumming. "I saw the buffalo dance," I said, sorry that it had ended. He nodded and his drum was gone. Instead, he picked up the medicine bag and hung it around my neck. "It has my semblance in it. A fetish, you know."

"Yes, I know. I used to have one of you when I was still a human. I always thought of it like maybe a telephone. I could hold it, scatter some cornmeal and bless it with my breath, and call you when I was in trouble."

"That is what I want you to use it for also here. Call me if you need help."

My whole being contracted in sudden disappointment. "You are not going to stay? I thought we would now stay together. That was one of my ideas of eternity and bliss." My voice choked. The pain was overwhelming.

"You are still a ghost," he said kindly. "There is much that you have to learn on your own before you can turn into a spirit, and I too have other tasks to attend to."

"And when will you be back?"

"Some Indian friends of mine who live north of here call this lunar period that of the Female Marmot. I'll try to be back when you see its last quarter in the sky." He saw that I was confused. I had no idea what a marmot looked like, neither Mother Marmot nor Father Marmot. That of course did not matter. But even more important, I was not even sure if I could tell exactly if it was the last quarter of the moon or not. So he added, "That will be in four days."

For a while we sat quietly, enjoying Ash Boy's modest flames. Then he said, "Cricket is coming. Let us go outside and share the food with our Animal Brothers."

Cricket had placed the clay pot close to the marigolds, and to eat, we sat around it in a circle, Brother Porcupine, Brother Badger, Sister Snake, and ourselves. The Animal People arrived as flecks of light and turned into their animal shapes while eating their first bite. Sometimes they looked like humans. The Messenger joined us last; he scampered up from the riverbed and was in such a hurry that he almost stumbled over his staff. The strange wolf, whom I had seen in the junipers, had come closer, crouching low, and now crowded in beside me. He was handsome, a white ruff set off by his gray fur, slightly pointed small ears, a black line drawn between them, and melancholy amber eyes.

"Tomorrow you may want to visit the Lower World," Buffalo was saying between gulps. "There are a number of things that you can learn there."

I thought I saw a fleeting shadow a little way up the hill, and apparently Brother Wolf saw it too, for he growled briefly and raised his hackles. I put my hand on his head for a moment, expecting him to give a little shake and turn into vibrating light, but he did not. And as the Moon of the Female Marmot rose above Stone Man Mountain, Buffalo gave a brief nod and was gone.

I was sitting in front of my house the next morning, getting ready to go to the Lower World, as Buffalo had suggested. The sky was an unearthly, intense blue. A foot-high whirlwind passed down below in the dry riverbed. I could see the faint outlines of a Spirit Person in it being carried along, a black-hooded face and a crown of yellow lightning, dancing on tiptoes and twirling around. It looked like fun. Cricket was nowhere to be seen or heard. Maybe she did not feel like going to the Lower World with me. I started to lie down in the requisite posture and was going to call my rattle when, unexpectedly, a Being rounded the left corner of my house. It had on a magnificent cape, all shimmering scales, the hood of which partly obscured its face. In the back, the cape had a bulge, as though draped over a tail. I sat up.

"So you are our new inhabitant?" the Being said in a rough, unpleasant male voice.

"Right."

"And you are Seed Bearer Woman."

I was startled. I did not know this stranger. "And what is your name?" I asked back.

"I have many names, more than you can remember. You are getting ready to go to the Lower World?"

I was getting tense. "How do you know all of that?"

"I am a Spirit Being. We are all omniscient. Of course, as a newcomer and ghost, you cannot be aware of that."

It sounded suspicious. I remembered my friend the Messenger insisting that there were "no omnis around here." I thought I had better break off the conversation when he continued: "Strange and dangerous place, that Lower World. There is a place where blood thirsty jaguars will tear you apart. There is a place where you will burn to ashes. And there are diseases all about, boils, bleeding, broken bones. It should be obvious to you that you need a knowledgeable guide. You are in luck. I can be your guide."

"Look," I said angrily, "I have been to the Lower World many times before, and saw no such thing. I don't need any guide. So maybe you should just leave."

I lay down, closed my eyes, and placing my left arm on my forehead, I was about to call my rattle, when I felt a tremendous weight bearing down on me. It was the stranger, who to my horror was now trying to do to me what a man does. I started screaming, "I am a ghost, I have no vagina! Let me be!" and tried to shake him off, but he was too heavy. Then I heard a growl; the stranger yelled in pain and got off me. I opened my eyes and saw a tall dark shadow: Grandfather Bear was standing right there, with the stranger dangling from his right paw. The would-be rapist was Old Man Coyote! His shimmering garment had fallen to the ground, Brother Wolf was trying to snap at his leg, and Cricket excitedly chimed and scolded.

"Dumb broad," Old Man Coyote was rasping. "We were going to have some fun, that's all."

"You mean you were going to. Did you ask her?"

"Let me go. You have no right to hold me like this!"

Grandfather Bear shook him again. "I am asking you: did you?"

"What for? She's only a ghost. Besides, I don't usually."

"We know that. Maybe you should start doing it more often." And Cricket chimed in, "And you lied to her. I know how you found out about her. I saw you last night in the bushes when we had supper. You omniscient? It's a laugh."

"Only a figure of speech. Everybody is entitled to some advertisement. So let me go."

Grandfather Bear put him down, and not very gently either. "Now apologize to her. And give her your cape as compensation."

"Not my cape!" Grandfather Bear's growl was unmistakable. "Oh, all right. But it isn't fair."

During all this conversation, I was writhing on the ground like a trampled ant. I finally was able to sit up, still trembling and feeling very cold. I nodded when, with a surly "sorry," Old Man Coyote dropped his shimmering garment in front of me, then slunk into an arroyo behind the stunted cottonwood tree one hill over.

Grandfather Bear stepped behind me and supported me with his strong and yet soft belly. He smelled of wild animal, and his voice was kind and reassuring. "He won't do it again," he said. "You are so cold. We'll do a healing, all right? Kneel for me; you are too shaky to stand."

"Call your rattle," the beloved voice of Holy Wind whispered. I rolled my fingers and placed them above my navel, then called my rattle: "Sound good, little sister, sound

sweet." Before I closed my eyes, I saw Sister Snake through my tears, and Brother Badger, and there was the Wolf, too, and Cricket on the tip of the juniper bush. "I am not alone," I thought thankfully.

The river and the junipers and the barren hills turned purple, and the sun was a softly glowing disk of gold. Grandfather Bear was still standing behind me, but I could also see him, and he was wearing a papier-maché mask with a black velvet nose. It looked comical. I had to laugh; my heart was beating very fast, and I was beginning to feel extremely hot. Grandfather Bear patted me on the head, and I turned into a little bear. "Let's run," he said, but then he changed into a rotating wheel of fire that I could not follow. A procession of deer walked along the crest of the hills; they turned into deer dancers, and their pulsating dance song resounded from a rock wall that arose behind them. I tried to follow them, but I was so tired I fell down, and Grandfather Bear leaned over me and with his soft, warm tongue he licked me all over. "Seed Bearer Woman," I heard from a distance, "Seed Bearer Woman!" The sound of my rattle had stopped, and I opened my eyes.

Grandfather Bear was gone. So was everyone else, except for Cricket, who was sitting on Old Man Coyote's cape, chiming contentedly.

"Feeling better?" she asked. I nodded. "Grandfather Bear is going to accompany you to the Lower World when he gets around to it," he said. I thought that was wonderful. I liked company. "Is Brother Wolf coming too?"

"I don't think so. But I found out something about him that you may want to know." I went over to my house and leaned against the adobe wall, warmed by the rays of the midday sun.

"In Old Pueblo, Brother Wolf lived," Cricket started out in the manner of a Pueblo tale. "He was selected to be one of the performers at a Kachina dance. The Old People told them that during the four days of the celebration they were not allowed to make love to any girl."

"And he did?"

"Right. On the third day. He thought nobody would know, but then his mask stuck to his face and he could not take it off. That way the people knew what he had done. He was ashamed, and so he died."

"He wore a wolf's mask?"

"No, he only appears that way around here."

Brother Wolf had trotted out of the bushes and was lying by the marigolds, his nose on his paws.

"How come he was not admitted to the Lake? I understood that there was no eternal punishment around here?"

"There isn't. He simply has not been invited in yet. They say there is a condition. The Wood Spirits need to like him. That has not happened. There is also something about feathers, but I don't know the details."

I was suddenly gripped by fear. What if the Wood Spirits

took a dislike to me too? What if after my forty days were over I would still not be allowed to go beneath the Lake? What then? I wished Buffalo were here so I could ask him these questions.

"So what is he going to do now? Can't he simply live here with you?"

I thought I heard an exasperated sigh in between my Sister Cricket's chime. "Can you imagine what that would be like? To live forever as a ghost with a mask stuck to your face? And no chance of ever becoming a spirit?"

Cricket attached herself to my hair. "Don't worry, something is bound to come along. It always does. So why don't we go and have some fun? Lift your arms and we'll fly along the old river."

And that was what we did. Off we flew, Cricket in my hair and Brother Wolf hanging onto my garment. I was happy that at least he did not decide to stay behind and mourn by himself. We passed some ancient junipers that were hanging on to the crumbling sandy bank by a single root as though by their big toe. One of them had a wrinkled old man's face. He was holding a gnarled rabbit club, but I saw no rabbit around. There was a large Apache war-bonnet bush spreading its branches above a sprawling sand bank and in each blossom the miniature face of a warrior. I blinked, and the faces were gone. Then we came to a spot where an arroyo cut into the riverbed at a sharp angle, and in its fold there was a clump of reeds. I folded my arms and we sank down right in front of it.

"Cricket, look! It cannot be. Reeds in the desert?" I went closer, parted the slender tall blades, and froze in total amazement. I was looking at the shimmering, sky-blue surface of a small, perfectly round lake, its calm surface disturbed only toward the back by the bubbles of the spring that was feeding it. To my left at its rim, almost hidden by the reeds, there stood an Indian elder by a clump of mountain bluebells, his face painted with vertical blue lines and dressed in a blue, silky pair of pants and a shirt embroidered with blue asters. In front of him there was a large drum with a leg attached and painted with the blue likeness of Avanyu, the Rain Serpent. At the very moment when I parted the reeds, he lifted his drumstick, and, to the rhythm of his drum, he started singing:

> Heya ho ho, heya ho,
> Avanyu's blue children
> Heya ho ho, heya ho,
> Children of the spring
> Rising.

With the first sound of the song, a young man rose out of the lake as though boosted up by the bubbles of the spring. He wore the customary kilt and a strap of cowry shells across his chest, which was painted blue; so were his arms and his face. He carried a blue rattle in one hand and in the other one a bunch of asters. He was followed by a girl in a white manta, wearing a beautiful tablita, a headdress painted with bluebirds facing an aster, and crowned by the drawing of a thin rain cloud, the rising sun, and three pyramids called kiva steps in the Pueblos. She was also painted blue and had a blue rattle. They were followed by five more couples, and as soon as each one emerged completely from the bubbles of the spring, they began dancing on the surface of the water to the sound of the elder's drum.

Trying not to move the reeds, I sat down and watched. Just like during a Pueblo dance in the ordinary world, they followed a well-rehearsed choreography, forming a straight line, then two circles, then merging once more, and each time they passed the elder, they raised their rattles and greeted him with a special fast signal. Four times they performed their dance, then they turned and one by one they sank below the surface of the lake over by the spring. When the last dancer had vanished, the elder picked up his drum and wanted to follow them, but at that moment Brother Wolf left my side and with a few bounds placed himself directly in front of him.

"Cricket," I said under my breath, "what is the meaning of this? What is Brother Wolf doing?"

Cricket did not answer. Instead, Holy Wind whispered in my ear: "Brother Wolf is telling Blue Water Grandfather that he was not admitted to the Large Lake. He says that he is weary of roaming around and would he let him enter the Blue Lake instead?"

We could see Blue Water Grandfather hesitating, as though he was considering the request. Then he said something I could not hear clearly, shook his head, picked up his drum, and in slow, old man's steps he walked across the shiny lake surface and sank into the spring, leaving Brother Wolf behind, whimpering dejectedly at the water's edge. "Blue Water Grandfather said that Brother Wolf offered no feathers, so there was no admittance," Holy Wind added. Cricket explained later that Brother Wolf had been looking for feathers all over but had not been able to find the special kind he needed.

Grandfather Bear did not come calling until the next afternoon, the day before Buffalo was to come again. I had been down in a deep arroyo. There was a huge rock there, all aglitter with fool's gold. Cricket enjoyed crawling under it and then I was to find it. But I preferred sitting on top of it, listening to the rock's hum. It was a song without words,

of age, and of timelessness, a brown-colored rumble that had the fragrance of wet earth about it.

After a while some noisy pinyon jays settled in a Russian olive tree nearby, telling each other the day's news, that charms of hummingbirds had come by on their way south and that those pesky bluebirds had arrived that ate everyone's food. Then I heard the familiar whispering in my ear. "Grandfather Bear has come," Holy Wind said. I called to Cricket, but she did not want to come along to the Lower World. "It's cold down there," she demurred. So after thanking Grandfather Stone for his song, I lifted my arms and landed next to my house. Grandfather Bear was indeed waiting by the marigolds. "Get your cape," he said; "the Lower World is a bit chilly."

To tell the truth, I had resolved never to touch that gift of compensation from Old Man Coyote, but there was no disregarding Grandfather Bear's suggestion. So I fetched it from the hanging beam in my house and, lying down, covered myself, placed my left arm on my forehead, and called my rattle.

I was caught in a whirlwind, and it threw me round and round. I was afraid I would become dizzy, but I smelled Grandfather Bear, then felt his arms around me, and we slipped into an endless dark tunnel together. The darkness dissolved into black, dancing rings. Then the rings turned a glowing yellowish green. I was traveling more slowly now, but still all was dark for a while, and I felt a cold draft on my chest. Visible only indistinctly, a huge cat opened its mouth; the faces of other animals appeared next to it, of a rabbit, then of a small mouse. Finally the sun came up, as if behind a dense fog. I was on a vast green plain, and in the grass there was a lovely boat, beige, with a blue pattern. Blue Water Grandfather would like that, I thought, but when I wanted to see it more closely, one of the blue Avanyu dancers appeared and folded it up like a sack. He lifted a staff and sparks flew in all directions; the sun was gone, it was dark again, and the sparks outlined a hole in the middle of the blackness. "Let's go through," Grandfather Bear said. The darkness on the other side was soft and had a reddish, velvety hue. To the right of me there was a low building, barely visible until I stepped up more closely and saw its shuttered back windows. A mighty sweet longing took hold of me. "I want to go in there in the worst way, Grandfather Bear," I said. "What is behind those shutters?" "Your grandmother's tavern," he said, "and your childhood. You cannot visit there until you've turned into a spirit." He took my hand and I was a hawk and flew low over the land. I passed into a gorge and a buzzard sat on a crag. He had a funny cap on crooked and he smiled, and I was no longer a hawk but a woman. Right behind him on a flat sandy plaza a group of girls was dancing; I heard no drum or song, and I could see only their reddish-brown skirts. In the middle of each skirt there was a fist-size turquoise. "Kachinas," Grandfather Bear's voice said. Sud-

denly I felt something touching my forehead and a shudder
passed down my back. "Buffalo has come," I exclaimed.
Grandfather Bear was gone; I found myself at the bottom of
a huge stairway hewn into the rock, and at the very top of
it a small domed doorway glowing in a vivid orange gold.
"Buffalo," I called, "Buffalo!" and I flew up the stairs and
crashed through the golden gate.

"What's your hurry, Seed Bearer Woman?" Buffalo said
in comic wonder as he lifted the cape off my supine form.

I sat up, still a bit groggy.

"You called me."

"Hey, your senses are pretty keen," he laughed. "For a
ghost, that is."

Later, when we sat once more in my house on the buffalo
skin in front of Ash Boy's fire, Buffalo started the conversation with the remark, "So you had a run-in with Old Man
Coyote?" I do not know if ghosts can blush, but it certainly
felt like I did.

"He is evil," I said angrily.

"You know that that is not true. We have no evil spirits
around here."

Of course I knew that, in theory. I had always taught it,
too. But it was a different matter when you came face to
face with such a devious, obscene being. "So how do you
account for him then?" I asked testily.

Buffalo had his drum in his hand. Thoughtfully, he tapped
out a slow rhythm, then started singing:

> Heya, heya, heya, ho
> All is dark
> Breath of Sky

All is dark above the waters
Heya, heya.

Heya, heya, heya, ho
All is dark
Power beings
All is dark above the waters
Heya, heya.

Heya, heya, heya, ho
All is dark
Earth from foam
All is dark above the waters
Heya, heya.

Heya, heya, heya, ho
All is dark
Earth weds sky
Old Man Coyot walks the clouds
Heya, heya.

Heya, heya, heya, ho
All is dark
Coyote stumbles
Old Man Coyot steals the sun
Heya, heya.

Heya, heya, heya, ho
All is bright
Beings dance
Old Man Coyot goes on stealing,
Heya, heya.

Buffalo finished the song with a brief laugh. I wanted to
comment that when I was a human, there was a lot of talk
about chaos theory, which I thought fitted right in with this
song about Old Man Coyote. But then the Spirits apparently knew all about that eons ago. So instead, still rever-

berating with Buffalo's song and its cosmic vision, I said nothing and only watched the flickering flame for a while. Then I told Buffalo about Brother Wolf and how Blue Water Grandfather would not admit him to his lake because he had no feathers to offer.

"He needs very special ones and they are hard to find," explained Buffalo. "Tell me," he asked, also looking at the flame, "why is it that you want to be admitted to the Lake?"

"When I was a little girl, my nursemaid told me what she thought heaven looked like, a flowery meadow and bird song, and everyone happy. That was where she wanted to go when she died. Maybe I think of the Lake that way, only a desert instead of a flowery meadow, with rabbit brush blooming, and the cicadas fiddling away."

"And elderly Pueblo Indians with wings of angels and a harp?" Buffalo teased. "Come, Seed Bearer Woman, let's go out. Cricket has brought our supper."

"Will you stay longer this time?" I asked over our blue cornmeal mush.

"That is not up to me."

I was confused. "You are very powerful, one of the First Beings, Cricket said. So isn't it your decision whether you come or go?"

Buffalo was patient. "It is another one of those rules," he said. "Beauty, harmony, balance, that was the original Dream. Without it life will cease. The problem is that humans keep destroying the balance."

"It's pretty hopeless, isn't it?"

"No, not really. But we need to work at it. Balance can be restored in ritual. We keep inviting humans to our side and give them rituals for exactly this purpose."

"So humans can't really invent rituals?"

"They can, of course, but not sacred ones. Those are

always gifts from the Spirit World. But for such a ritual to be effective, humans and Spirits need to perform it together. When humans call us to participate in a ritual, we are obligated to go."

"So when you suddenly leave, that is where you go?"

"Usually."

"And here I thought that the Messenger was being unnecessarily pompous when he said that you were unavoidably detained. He was right!"

"You'd better apologize to him the next time you see him," Buffalo smiled.

We had flown up almost to the top of Stone Man Mountain in the late afternoon sunshine after supper, Buffalo, Cricket, Brother Wolf, and I, and were sitting among the slender, velvety gray stems of a grove of aspens. A light wind shuddered high above through the foliage.

"You may suddenly be gone again, like the last time," I said, turning to Buffalo. "If that is the case, when will you be back?"

One of the delicate leaves, turned to gold by the breath of fall, settled on my hair. Buffalo picked it off, and looking at it, he said slowly, "It will be time for the new moon in a few days. The Arikara call this lunar period The One In Which the Leaves Fall. Expect me at the new moon." He stepped in among the aspens and was gone.

A deer mouse with a white waistcoat and glittering black eyes under big round ears was skittering through the dry leaves. "Somebody is coming," it squeaked.

We turned toward the rustling noise some distance away. It can only be the Messenger, I thought, and indeed, his round form soon approached, all green and shiny, pushing through the tall brown grasses.

"I have a message," he puffed. "A most important per-

sonage, she has come for a visit. She is waiting for you in
your house. Hurry, hurry!"

"Are you coming too?" I asked as I gathered Cricket into
my hair and motioned to Brother Wolf to hang on.

But he shook his head. "No, actually, I have a fear of
flying. Besides, I have to report her safe arrival. Hurry!"

As I lifted my arms to fly, I wondered to whom he might
have to report and especially who the important visitor
might be.

I looked around when we came to rest by the marigolds,
but there wasn't anybody around. I climbed up the ladder,
and seeing no one on the roof, I started down through the
hatch hole: no visitor. The slanting light of evening illumi-
nated only a magnificent spider whom I had not noted
before, who was spinning her web in the corner. Her legs,
moving gracefully along the strands, were the color of sand
and edged in white bristles. They were banded with stripes
of brown and orange. The lower part of her body was a
pinkish brown, fading upward into a creamy white and
bearing the design of a corn plant. I could not see her head
because it was half obscured by a small bundle that I took
to be her infants, which spiders are wont to carry with them
before they release them into the world.

"Good evening, Grandmother Spider," I said politely.

At the sound of my voice she seemed to stiffen; the busy
movement of her legs ceased, and she did something I
remembered from Cricket, only in reverse. Cricket had
pulled her black garment over her body of light from the
back to show me her cricketness, while the spider stripped
her furry garment back and what emerged was not a flickering light but a slender, rather tall, gray-haired Indian
woman in an embroidered shift, holding a shopping bag.

"Olah, younger sister," she said.

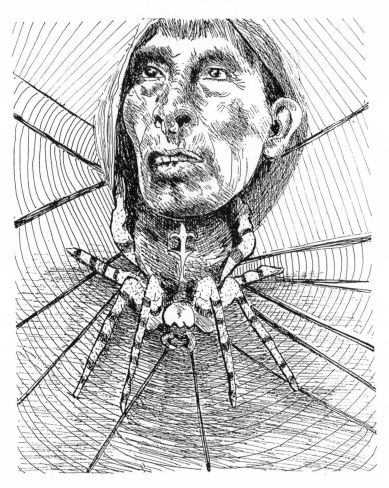

I hung on to the ladder so I would not sink down in a faint. "Usa?" I finally asked, not believing what I saw. She nodded. Usa, my beloved Maya friend, the only person ever to call me "younger sister." She had died years ago and my life had not been complete since.

"I was told that you had no hammock," she said in her determined way, which I remembered so well, "so I brought you one." She pulled it out of her shopping bag and expertly knotted its ropes over the crossbeams. Then she spread its silky threads, an invitation for me to sit down.

So there I sat, facing her, with the hammock forming a love seat, and still at a loss for words. "Usa," I said finally, "how—"

"I had heard rumors," she smiled. "It was said that you had arrived. I made a request; I wanted to visit you. But of course it was refused. You know, the men."

"So you snuck out?"

"Not exactly. There was that little bell, on top of a deserted section of the wall." Things were beginning to fall into place. Cricket had been to Yucatan with me. She knew about Usa. No wonder that several times I had looked for her in vain.

"What did the little bell suggest?"

"That there was this Grandmother Spider, who was very powerful, a sort of witch, you know, and if I had the courage, I could slip into her garment. No one would have to know." I suddenly knew to whom the Messenger had to go and report Usa's arrival!

"Thank you, Cricket," I said toward the corner, where I had heard her chime in a crack in the clay wall. I thought I heard a tiny titter.

It was a good thing that ghosts and spirits needed no sleep, for we frittered the whole night away. "I knew that you had made friends with the Grandfathers and so would not come to our place." "How did you discover that? You would have nothing to do with the world of the Grandfathers, pledging allegiance to the new message instead. I always kept it a secret so I would not hurt your feelings." She laughed that throaty laugh of hers. "I saw you through the lattice of my kitchen one day when you ate breakfast. You scattered a small offering, and the Grandfathers came." I was amazed. "You saw them?" "No, but my cat did. She started toward you, she lifted her paws carefully so she would make no noise, and her eyes were glowing coals." "You said nothing." "I did not want to hurt your feelings either."

"And what is it like, I mean at your place?" Usa slowly rocked the hammock.

"No marauding soldiers. I have finally been able to forget what burned human flesh smells like. No worries and no hunger. No illness or pain."

"Do you get to see many strangers? I thought perhaps my mother? She died when I was young."

"No, I don't think so. She is probably in another section. We are mostly by ourselves. Although many of those arriving have not been properly baptized. You know, not by immersion, merely by a little water on their heads. I like to go over and gossip with them, though, about their lives, things like that. But the men do not approve."

"So how about the men? Has your husband arrived?"

"He has, finally. He was always slow." We both laughed.

"It took him half a day to buy one fried fish on the market," I reminisced.

"And of course he joined the game of the men. Only they are more polite about it now: No, dear brother, I belong on a higher cloud than you. Actually, dear brother, I think you may be wrong; when I was still a human, as you will recall—" she grinned mischievously.

"Do you miss anything?"

"The smells of the market, maybe. My flowers. And the animals. No animals at all, no songbirds, no pheasants, no deer, no turkeys. Not even a piglet. Most of all the feel of earth on my hands. They won't let me make a garden."

I laid my hand next to hers, as we used to do on our interminable bus rides. Mine was chubby and white, hers brown, gracefully slender, narrower than mine and longer.

It was a wordless declaration of affection. We smiled at each other in mute remembrance.

"Let's make a garden then," I suggested.

We went outside and she chose a flat spot close to my house. It was bare, with only a single prickly pear growing in one corner. She had a coarse henequen bag in her hand, and she reached in and brought out some seeds and a small stick. As I watched her bending down to make a hole in the sand, there was a curious distortion. In a most subtle manner she changed. She was Usa, but at the same time she was surrounded, enveloped, by a perceivable and yet invisible aura of Grandmother Spider, very real but at the same time ephemeral.

Totally absorbed, Usa dropped four kernels of corn into each one of the six holes she had dug, then she planted some black beans and two flat, large, white squash seeds in a circle around each corn hole. "Done," she nodded, being very much Usa. "It isn't much, but it is something." This was what she used to say when we were both still humans. But she did not remain Usa for long. She began humming, a delicate drum signal arose from among the clay clods, then she started singing, and once again that spirit-animal aura of hers was back, and she was not quite the Usa I had known:

> Wana, wana, wana-oh.
> In the red morning
> their mother dresses them.
> Beautifully she dresses them,
> the three sisters.
>
> Wana, wana, wana-oh.
> In the small garden
> they grow tall.
> Corn sister, squash sister, bean sister,
> the three sisters grow.

As she sang, the tightly furled corn leaves, the juicy cotyledon of the squashes, and the first two whorls of the beans, bearing their split mother on their humped backs, began breaking through the soil and stretching upward. Another instant and Usa's planting was a verdant garden patch in the brown desert.

"Now I want to take a bath," she said. That was right: a bath; every evening and sometimes in between, there had to be a bath at her place.

"I am afraid," I demurred, "I cannot offer you a bath. You know, I am only a ghost."

She was not listening. Instead she performed a round motion with her hand, and there was the flat willow skeleton of a sweat lodge. Another movement, and it was covered with skins, leaving a low entryway to the east. Yet another one, and glowing stones rolled into the opening. Usa was gone, the entrance was closed, and from the inside of the sweat lodge there came the hissing sound of water turning to steam, the fragrance of sage, and prayer fragments, Mother Earth, Father Sky, Grandfather Fire, Wind of the North, Wind, Wind, and in the whispering of the steam, the answer of Mother Earth, speaking to her daughter.

All of a sudden, the sweat lodge was no more, and wriggling out of its fire pit from among the blackened rocks there emerged the yellowish-pink spider, the glowing design of the corn plant on her back, bearing her small bundle and climbing upward on a single silky green thread that stretched up high, as though attached to the very cupola of the sky. She grew ever smaller, then she was gone, and in her place a round gilded cloud appeared next to the setting sun, and from it, to the north, the east, the south, and the west, the spokes of a giant spiderweb spread over the entire sky, a celebration of Grandmother Spider's cosmic grandeur.

"What is the matter with you?" asked Cricket in between her gay little chimes. "You have been moping and moping ever since Usa left. Ghosts are supposed to be happy, you know."

We had spent the night riding around on soft furry bats, screeching with mirth and hanging on with all our might so we would not be left behind. How fast they were, darting hither and thither! But they had left at the first sign of the morning's early light to go hang upside down in an old barn back in the hills, they said. They wanted us to come along, but I didn't feel like it. Without warning, all my exhilaration had escaped out of me like air out of a pricked balloon. The reality was that Usa had left.

"Moping again," Cricket repeated. We were up in the Jemez Mountains among some burst and fractured tree trunks, blackened by a recent forest fire. The ground was black, too; only at one place was there a spot of yellow. When I looked closer, it turned out to be a small fragment of ochre that a passerby might have lost here. "Look, how pretty," I said to Cricket, as I picked it up and playfully passed it from one hand to the other and then put it in my pocket. A breeze started up, announcing the arrival of the Dawn Boys and Dawn Maidens. As they rushed by, they waved to us, but they would not stop to socialize; they had to run fast on their golden yellow moccasins, their long black hair flying, so Father Sun's rays would not catch them.

"Usa simply left," I said, swinging on a dry branch that was going "creek, creek" in the breeze left behind by the dawn runners.

"She had to. Grandmother Spider was calling her. With

Grandmother Spider, you do as you are told. Besides, she would have been missed at home. They are not really nice at her place. 'You do that and we will see to it that you end up in hell,' I heard somebody yell when I was spying on that wall. Whatever hell is, it probably isn't nice."

"She could at least have said something like 'God bless you' in parting, the way she used to."

"I am sure she knew that that would have been inappropriate around here."

"I saw her being hauled up into the sky. Maybe she is still there. Let's go up, all right? At least I could try to find her and say farewell to her. Will you come along?"

"Anything," said Cricket and it sounded almost like a sigh. "You are no fun when you are in this mood."

I found a hillock with the right kind of incline, stretched down on it and adjusted my arms to the required posture, left arm straight, right arm loose. Cricket tried to hide on my left hand first, but that was too stiff, so she crawled into the folds of my right palm. I called my rattle sister, closed my eyes, and we were off.

I was jolted by a beam of light; it lifted me up, and it was an eagle. It swallowed me and I could see out through its eyes. It circled over the land; we were above a lake, and I could see the eagle's shadow reflected by its gleaming surface. Then we were above a high plain; the sun was shining, and there were two figures in a light green sleeping bag, their bodies curving outward, outlined under the cover. Next to their heads on either side there were a pair of tall antlers, as though they had taken them off like a feather bonnet before going to bed.

I do not remember whether the eagle spit me out, but suddenly there I was in a huge mountain range of majestic yellow and pink clouds. Emerging from the side of one of the mountains there were rainbows, one following the other like an avenue of arched gates, and I darted in and out of them; and as I touched them, each had a different sound, reverberating together as one giant celestial harp. Then I was propelled even higher, and I saw the earth; it was sparkling and surrounded by a wreath of dancing spirits. But I don't want to see the earth, I cried out, I want to see Usa! So I began to sink and sink, deeper, ever deeper into the clouds. There was a path; I followed it, and there between two rocks, a spider's eyes glinted at me. "Do not go any closer," Holy Wind whispered into my ear. But I took a large step anyway. "Usa," I called, stretching out my arms, "farewell, farewell!" I took one more step, the clouds gave way, and through a hole, I tumbled head over heels into the precipitous depth.

For the longest time there was only darkness and nothing. Then from far away I heard my dear little Cricket, and her usually merry bell sounded mournful, as though she were sobbing. "Cricket," I sighed, "Cricket, where are you?" The darkness gradually cleared, and I was back on the hillside among the scorched trees. Cricket was sitting on my chest, a heaving little glob of light.

"What happened?" I asked, folding my arms under my head.

"That was something very foolish you did there," she scolded. "You should not have approached Grandmother Spider."

"That was Usa," I insisted, and triumphantly I added, "and I did say farewell to her."

"And you might have been killed. Others falling through a hole in the sky did not survive it. That is what the stories teach. There was the sky chief's daughter; she pulled up a sacred tree that smelled like a turnip, and she fell through the hole and died. And there was the girl who married the Sun; she quarreled with him and dug a hole through the sky, fell down, and died. And then there was the girl who married the Morning Star; she also had marital problems, and—" Cricket ran out of breath.

"But I have already died. I cannot die again, can I?"

"Yes, you can. Ghosts are not immortal. Only spirits are. And to tell you the truth, I have no idea how come you are still alive."

I sat up, feeling pretty shaky. As I did so, I felt Buffalo's medicine bag warm against my chest.

"I think I know why," I said, holding it up.

Cricket nodded. "I'm sure you're right. Come on, let's fly home."

I stood up and lifted my arms, but nothing happened: I could no longer fly. I tried again, the required four times, with the same result. I had the feeling that all my strength had left me. Cricket was so startled she did not utter a sound. Cricket not chiming, that was truly frightening.

"Call Buffalo for help," my whispering Voice suggested.

My shaky legs refused to support me, so I sat down once more, loosened the medicine bag from my neck, and took out the delicately carved buffalo fetish. As I placed it on my left palm, its yellow heart line glowed as a thing alive. I breathed on it and prayed. "Mighty Buffalo, powerful older brother, hear me, take pity on me. I have lost my strength. I cannot fly. Please, come and help me."

The sky above us assumed its most intense blue. A dark cloud briefly obscured the light of the sun, and it assumed the shape of a buffalo, bearing the sun between its horns. The vision dissolved, and Buffalo stepped out from the thicket behind the scorched trees.

"So you lost your strength, Seed Bearer Woman?" There was no criticism, no reproach, only a simple statement of fact. Dispirited, I could only nod.

"Can you help me, please, Buffalo?" I finally asked.

"I cannot, but I can accompany you to some powerful healers. I am sure they will be able to do something for you if we ask them in the proper way." And anticipating my complaint that I could no longer fly, he added, "Come, I'll take you on my back." He turned, and in his place there stood the dark brown buffalo I had so often seen in my visions. The next thing I knew, I was straddling his back with Cricket in my hair. We lifted off and crossed over Frijoles Canyon, where unimaginably mighty forces once rent the crust of the earth asunder, and then over the next one where the lightning of spirit power had struck me so many years ago and forever changed my life. Buffalo turned toward the left, and we gradually descended to a place I was very familiar with from photographs, the Sanctuary of the Stone Lions. When I was still a human, I once set out to see this famous sacred place, but my strength gave out before I got there, and I had to turn back.

So finally here I was, gazing in awe at the fence of interlocking bleached antlers left as offerings and behind it the sandy colored stone outcroppings that an ancient artist had fashioned into the likeness of two smiling mountain lions. But there was a tremendous surprise, and I told Buffalo about it as I slipped off his back and he was in his human form once more.

"In my visions just now, when I traveled to the Sky World," I tried to explain, "I saw this sanctuary. Or some form of it, maybe. But I didn't recognize it. What I saw was two figures in what I thought was a shimmering light green sleeping bag, and they had antlers next to them, and they were curved toward each other just like these Stone Lions."

"You needed to come to see them," he nodded; "that was already known. And they are so powerful that in disguise they intruded into your space. Present is both future and past, as you know." He took my hand and said, "Come, let us greet them."

We picked our way over the antlers, and as we approached the stone figures, they began to vibrate and emitted a greenish light, the same color as the sleeping bag that I had seen. They rose and stretched catlike, then shook themselves and were balls of light.

"Mountain Lions, Mountain Lion people, mighty healers," Buffalo said quite casually, "we come to greet you and to ask you for a healing." The lights shook themselves and were not mountain lions now, but a man and a woman. They wore eagle feathers in their long black hair, and they were draped in a mountain lion skin that fell down in soft folds, as I had once seen a medicine man wear it at a Pueblo winter dance.

"This ghost has lost her strength," Buffalo continued. "Foolishly, she stepped through a hole in the sky, that was how it happened."

The mountain lion people looked me over for what seemed a long time. Then the mountain lion woman said, in a voice that sounded like the wind rustling in the gorges, "Lie down, my daughter, we will heal you."

There was a buff skin on the ground within the antler enclosure; it was inclined at the angle required for a trip to the upper world by invisible forces, and I lay down on it, adjusted my arms as before and closed my eyes.

A drum started up with a fast beat, then the mountain lion pair began singing, "aha, aya, ayaho." I thought they were also dancing, but I could not check on that because I was back in the clouds, seeing the spider's eyes once more. "Do not go any closer," I heard the whisper of Holy Wind. This time I listened. Sadly, because I could not say farewell to Usa, I retraced my steps, then sat down on a cloud. It carried me away, and when I opened my eyes, I was lying on the ground once more near the Stone Lions in the antler enclosure, with Buffalo offering his hand so I could stand up.

"Thank you, Mountain Lions, Mountain Lion People, mighty healers," I said, turning to the stone figures. "Your blessing I will return to you." Then remembering the fragment of ochre I had picked up at the place of the burned trees, I took it and reverently painted their rough ancient faces with it.

Once more we were sitting in front of Ash Boy's fire in my house, Buffalo and I. I had had no problems flying home.

"What exactly happened?" Buffalo asked.

I told him the details and then added, "It was a curious kind of healing, as though they caused the film of the events to run backwards."

"That was not exactly what they did," Buffalo explained. "You see, with your impulsive action, which caused you to disregard the warning of Holy Wind, you had created a disturbance in the cosmic order, endangering its balance and its beauty. So with their power, they took you back to where your misstep started, to give you a chance to do it differently. You did do that, and in that way the delicate fabric of the cosmic order was repaired."

"See what a dummy you were?" a little voice said in my ear, and from its lilt it was clear that it was not Holy Wind speaking.

"I did give the Stone Lions my ochre to reciprocate for their gift of healing. Do you think that a prayer stick would also please them?" I asked.

Buffalo seemed to think about it. "Feathers are the garments of the Spirits," he said, "so that would be welcome. But you would need paint for the stick, yellow, blue, white, and red."

"I'll get her some from Grandmother Spider," volunteered Cricket.

"And the feathers need to be tail feathers of live birds."

"Maybe we could find some in the eastern riverbed," I suggested; "that is where they sometimes drop them when they descend to drink."

Buffalo thought that was a good idea, but when we went outside, there was Brother Wolf, looking quite dejected. He had been gone when we took the trip to the Stone Lions, so I had had no chance to ask him to come along.

"That is not the reason," said Buffalo. "He has been searching for feathers, but he has had no luck because with his mask still stuck to his face and having to look through his wolf-mask eyes he cannot see very well."

"Well then, Brother Wolf," I said, "come along with us. We are looking for feathers too."

Buffalo took Brother Wolf on his arms and together we flew east, but when we got to the river, there apparently had been some rain in the high country, for it had several small, clear arteries of water hurrying north, with deceptively solid-looking sandy stretches in between. "I remember what this river is like when it has water," I laughed, "it is a sticky mess. I once tried to hike in it. The mud kept sucking in my boots, and I arrived in the next Pueblo more dead than alive. It was only four miles away, but it took me four hours. I don't think we will find any feathers in it today."

"Let's try anyway. Maybe it is drier farther down river," said Buffalo. So we flew south, which was vastly superior to hiking in the wet mud, but saw no feathers anywhere. We finally got to a spot where the riverbed curved left below a red rock wall. It was riddled top to bottom with holes, and a multitude of busy swallows kept flying in and out. We descended and looked around.

"Do you have any tail feathers?" Buffalo called to one of the swallows as it was darting by.

"Maybe behind the rock," twittered the swallow, and it hurried on with a graceful swoop.

So we made our way through the cottonwood thicket and had just gotten to a clearing when I perceived, intermingled with the smell of moist earth, the intense fragrance of Douglas spruce. "Do you smell that, Buffalo?" I asked. "Where does that come from? Douglas spruce do not grow here."

Buffalo smiled and in Indian fashion pointed toward the other side of the clearing with his lips. I followed the direction of his signing, and almost obscured by some willows there was a small lake, tinted an intense yellow. What Buffalo had been pointing to was a shape that unexpectedly began rising out of the water, which did not even ripple as that Being noiselessly emerged, infinitely delicate like a soap bubble, not corporeal, but rather as if an invisible master painter were in the process of drawing its outline in the air against the backdrop of the cottonwood thicket. The sketch completed, it was a masked dancer with wavy black lines over his chest and arms. With his emergence, the intense smell of wet earth wafted over us like the blessing of a secret ritual. He disappeared behind the rock, apparently traveling south. Close behind him there arose another silent dancer, equally transparent, wearing a heavy collar of twigs of Douglas spruce, and upon his passing, the entire clearing was permeated with the scent of his wreath. Then came a dancer with a deer mask, deer hoofs strung on a leather strap across his chest, and spreading about him the smell of wild ruminants, and close up behind him an ephemeral shape all green, with sprigs of yellow marigolds on his mask, exuding their pungent fragrance. Then followed another one, equally green, with a wreath of speckled blossoms which I did not recognize. "Fragrant Spirits," I whispered to Buffalo, thinking the filmy parade was over. But Buffalo shook his head, and he was right, for rising from the calm waters two more transparent shapes appeared in close succession. One was a macaw, its red feathers glinting, and as I watched, it kept changing, sometimes into a bird, then again into a bird dancer flapping his wings, and after him came a most curious fellow. He was smaller than the others, seemed to be limping in moccasins too big for his feet, and fastened to the temples of his mask he wore bunches of the large white trumpet flowers of the thorn apple, the giver of dreams. He was the last one, but even after the passage of the gossamer parade, the clearing continued being permeated by the essence of their substance, like the fragrance of burned sage clinging to the kiva walls after a smudging.

"They live beneath the lake," I said, more a comment than a question. Buffalo nodded. "They are ancient spirits who chose not to be manifested in tangible shape," he said, "Summer beings who are being called to a ritual at the Pueblo."

Across from us, on the other side of the yellow lake, there was a male willow, and unexpectedly a yellow finch, sitting on one of its stiff branches, began to sing, breaking the silence with a succession of warbling flute tones. Then we heard a drumbeat, and a very old man started rising out of the yellow water as though he were climbing the ladder out of the kiva. First his gray head with a yellow scarf bobbed up, then his face bearing vertical yellow stripes, and finally all of him attired in a yellow shirt with sunflowers embroidered on it, and yellow silk pants. He was carrying a heavy drum with a stand strapped to it. The drum was painted with the yellow likeness of Avanyu, the Rain Serpent. He stopped on the edge of the lake to the left of us, and continuing to hit his drum, he began singing.

> Heya ho ho, heya ho
> Avanyu's yellow children,
> Heya ho ho, heya ho
> Children of the yellow lake
> rising.

At the last cadence of the song, dancers began breaking the surface of the lake, six pairs in all, in every detail duplicates of the dancers of the Blue Lake, down to the picture of Avanyu, the Rain Serpent, painted on the kilts of the young men, but everything was yellow. They were carrying yellow sunflowers in addition to their rattles, and drawings

of small yellow sunflowers instead of blue asters decorated the tablitas, the headdresses of the girls.

I looked at Buffalo. Beautiful, his approving smile seemed to say. Together we followed the intricate choreography, the lines dissolving into circles and spirals, and lines again. After the fourth time, the dancers returned to the spot where they had risen from the water and one after the other they sank below.

Only Brother Wolf, who had placed himself between Buffalo and myself to watch the dance, had not shared in our quiet enjoyment. He was restless, sitting down, getting up again, obviously anxious for the dancers to be done. And when they had left and Yellow Water Grandfather made ready to pick up his drum to follow them, he started up as he had done when we had encountered Blue Water Grandfather and placed himself in front of the venerable elder. The way Yellow Water Grandfather first hesitated and then shook his head, I did not need Holy Wind's explanation to understand that once more his request for asylum had been denied. No feathers, no entrance, it seemed.

I thought that this might be an opportunity for me to ask Buffalo about my own chances for eventually being admitted to the Large Lake. After all, half of my allotted forty days had already passed and I really wanted to find out about what was going to happen to me. But when I turned to him, he said, "The first quarter of this lunar period is over and I need to leave." And stirring the dry grass with the tip of his foot, he added, "Appropriately, our Pima friends call the upcoming full moon the Moon of the Dry Grass. Look for me at the time when it rises in the sky."

I was anxious to start on the prayer stick for the Stone Lions after Buffalo's departure. Making something beautiful I thought might help me get over the sadness that always took hold of me when he left. We went down to the riverbed once more, Cricket and I, and we coaxed Brother Wolf to come along too. He seemed more dejected than ever after his unsuccessful encounter with Yellow Water Grandfather. "Don't worry," I kept telling him, "I am sure you are going to find the right feathers one of these days." But I had the impression he was not even listening.

We found the stick I was looking for growing straight up from a cottonwood bush. "Please let me have this branch of yours," I explained to the cottonwood. "I need to make a prayer stick, and you know, pinyons and junipers do not grow any straight branches." The cottonwood sister nodded, and thanking her, I tore off the branch. She let it go easily because I think she was pleased about the compliment. I should have left some cornmeal too, but I didn't have any. I was feeling sorry for myself: Spirits received cornmeal from their humans, but as a ghost I was not entitled to such offerings.

"Now I'll go get you the paint from Grandmother Spider," Cricket said. "Or would you like to come with me?"

Of course I wanted to. We left Brother Wolf by the marigolds, where instead of searching for feathers he was sleeping his woes away, and flew toward the region where Cricket knew Grandmother Spider was staying at the moment, at her home in the shadow of Shimmering Mountain.

We were about halfway there when Cricket said unexpectedly, "Do you have anything that you can give Grandmother Spider for the paint?"

I was embarrassed. I had never even thought of that. So evasively I said, "You know about ghosts. We don't have anything. Do you have any suggestions?"

"You might give her a song."

"A song? I don't know any songs."

"Yes, you do. When you were still a human, you used to sing to me, 'I hear you, little Cricket Spirit. Thank you for singing for me.' That was a song. And I liked it."

I thought about possible songs the rest of the way, rejecting one poetic phrase after the other and hoping for a special inspiration when the need arose.

I did not have much time, for in the blink of an eye we arrived at the foot of Shimmering Mountain, the northern border of this land. We found Grandmother Spider busily working on an iridescent green web between two ponderosa pines, the fragrance of which was everywhere.

"You have come," she called from high above.

"We have a request," Cricket said.

Grandmother Spider angled down, and suddenly her eight long legs were gone and she was standing there in front of us, an old-fashioned Pueblo grandmother with a wonderfully wrinkled kindly face, her white hair cut straight across her forehead, wearing a loose yellow dress with pink flowers under a black manta, cinched by a tightly woven Hopi belt and richly beaded moccasins with black strouds. And the jewelry she wore! Long earrings, a heavy squash-blossom necklace, rings on every finger, and a Zuni needlepoint bracelet, all in silver and the most fabulous turquoise, blue-green with delicate spiderweb patterns.

"What do you want, my girl?" she asked, obviously amused at my frank admiration.

"We need paint," Cricket answered in my stead. And by way of an explanation, I added, "I want to tie a prayer stick for the Mountain Lions in return for their healing."

Grandmother Spider nodded. It was clear that she knew all about my misadventure and was not going to dwell on it. She stepped over to where a thick sage bush was growing and began singing softly, while from in between the pines a delicate drumbeat arose to accompany her:

> Aya, aya, aya-a-a
> Younger sister of the north
> Your gift of blue
> Aya, aya.

Miraculously, a small clay pot with a zigzag pattern painted on it and containing blue paint appeared on her outstretched hand. She placed it on the ground, and sang once more:

> Aya, aya, aya-a-a
> Younger sister of the west

Your gift of yellow
Aya, aya.

Once more a small pot appeared, this time with yellow paint. Then with her high voice like the trill of birds, she sang:

Aya, aya, aya-a-a
Younger sister of the south
Your gift of red
Aya, aya.

And a pot of red paint joined the line of the others. Finally she addressed the Spirit of the remaining direction:

Aya, aya, aya-a-a
Younger sister of the east
Your gift of white
Aya, aya.

And she placed a small pot containing white paint in a line with the rest. Then she spread a scarf the colors of the rainbow on the ground, put the four little paint pots on it, knotted it, and gave it to me.

"Thank you, Grandmother Spider," I said, and seeing Cricket anxiously lighting off and on the packet by way of a reminder, I added, "May I sing you a song in return?"

Perhaps because of her kind, grandmotherly presence, I was suddenly overcome by a deep longing, by a homesickness I rarely allowed myself to surrender to. From far away the breeze carried the echoes of a Hungarian shepherd's flute, and I sang to these long-forgotten strains:

Daughter of the distant plains
Blue forget-me-not, blue forget-me-not
My friends are weeping at my grave
Blue forget-me-not, blue forget-me-not.

Grandmother Spider put her arm around my shoulder. Then she said, "Thank you, my girl. I accept your song. It is beautiful." Then in quick succession she spit medicine on me, my head, my shoulders, my arms, even Cricket got a tiny drop, and smiling that wonderful ironic smile that Usa also had, she added, "To keep you safe on the way home." And then she was up in her web once more, a spider spinning along.

We should have gone straight back to the house with our bag of paints, but Cricket was feeling adventurous, and, of course, I had no feathers yet. So Cricket suggested that instead we fly south first, toward Turtle Mountain. "The summer birds cross there on their way back to Mexico," she said; "we may find some of their tail feathers on one of the crests."

For some reason, I felt apprehensive. As a human, I had often seen the crags and precipices of Turtle Mountain from the airplane, and that was not particularly inviting country. If we ever dropped down there because of an accident, I had often thought, nobody but nobody would come out alive. Now, of course, we could fly in and out of those frightening crevasses with impunity, and Cricket was in an especially playful mood. "Come on, Seed Bearer Woman." She rarely called me by my full name. "Come on, this is fun!"

Suddenly I could not hear her anymore. Where was she? I flew a little higher to have a wider view, and there, stretching far to the horizon, I saw a very high gray wall and in front of it a male figure all in black making a motion as though catching a fly.

"Got ya," I heard him shout, "got ya, you pesky thing. I've seen you here before, spying, that's what you're doing.

Here, take this!" He had Cricket in his fist and was trying to squash her.

"Cricket," I screamed, "come on!"

"I can't, he is sticky!"

I flew closer. "Watch it," Holy Wind warned, "this is dangerous!"

But I had to get Cricket. So I swooped directly against the man's hand. He was so startled he opened his fist and Cricket jumped up high and escaped into my hair.

"You!" he shouted furiously, grabbing my arm. "I know about you! You emigrated; it was all illegal! Now I'll take you in where you belong." He was beginning to shake me hard. "For your immortal soul, you need to be rescued, even if I have to kill you to do it!"

"Pull," Holy Wind said, "pull!" So that was what I did, and apparently Grandmother Spider's medicine had made me so slippery that our assailant could not keep hold of me, and my arm slid out of his grip.

"It's all right," Cricket chirped in my hair, "settle down; he can't go very far."

So I flew to a ponderosa close by, and while the black figure continued jumping up and down by the wall, shouting very impolite invectives, I sat down in the grass. "What happened, Cricket?"

Cricket sounded a little embarrassed. "I thought I saw a feather next to the wall, but it was only a shadow."

"He could have killed you."

"No. I am a spirit, remember, not a ghost." Cricket sometimes liked to rub that in. "But he could have held me prisoner. I have heard of such cases. Terrible." The tiny glob of light was visibly shuddering. "He is sticky, that fellow. But Grandmother Spider's medicine made me good and slippery."

"And what is behind that wall?"

"I only got a good look once, but it seemed like bubbles."

"Bubbles?"

"Right. Lots and lots of empty bubbles. And more of those black-coated guys wading through them. They seem perfectly happy there, singing along."

Cricket seemed to be giggling. "Just singing along in a sea of bubbles." Then she suggested that we fly along the wall a bit—not too close, of course—because there was something else she wanted me to see.

We flew for a while (it was apparently a very long wall), then we heard a kind of tapping, not a drumbeat but a dull irregular thud as if someone were pounding a very hard object with a rubber hammer. And rounding a bend, we saw who was making that sound. It was a man in a gray business suit, white shirt, and black tie, standing on top of the wall and hitting it with a plastic pickax. He was turned in our direction, and I was startled because he had no face. None. Only a blank oval sheet of paper in place of a face under a well-groomed toupee.

"Who is that?" I asked.

"We don't really know. We call him Harry Nothing Face."

"And what is he doing?"

"Mosquito Man once went on an excursion around here. He said that Harry Nothing Face gave him to understand that he was trying to develop the wall. But the wall did not seem to want to change."

We watched him hack away for a while, but it was very tedious, so we decided to fly home. Clearly this was not a very good place to look for feathers.

"Now what?" I asked Cricket as we were taking it easy at home next to the marigolds.

"I have heard the Old People tell that if you can't find any feathers, the birds will even give you some if you invite them properly."

"You know how?"

"Let me think. We need something to spread on the ground, and then we need to sing."

"Oh no! I don't know any songs like that."

"You didn't do too bad for Grandmother Spider. This song starts up high, then you go sort of halfway down, and then at the very end you go down completely and pull on the tone." Cricket demonstrated, and the strange description fit the melody exactly right. I had always thought Indian songs impossibly difficult to remember, but this way I could see it, like a lovely decorative line on a clay pot, which made learning it easier. "My voice is too weak," Cricket said. "The birds may not hear me, but if you sing along with me, we should do all right."

So I went and got my coyote cape from my house and spread it on the ground. Then Cricket started, scattering some cornmeal: "Ohey, ohey, ohey yaya." And bumping my nose, she chimed, "Come on, don't be bashful!" So I joined:

> Ohey, ohey, ohey yaya,
> Bird Spirits about
> We beg for feathers
> Ohey ya.

We repeated it the proper four times, but nothing happened. "You need to sing louder," Cricket scolded.

"No, I don't think that's it. We need a drum. When Buffalo sings, he always makes one appear, but I don't have that kind of power."

I looked around to see if there was anything that we

could use for a drum when who should come by but Old Man Coyote and, yes, he was carrying a drum. I was never going to speak to him again, but this was an emergency.

"I see you have a drum," I said cautiously. "Can I borrow it?"

"No."

"Please?"

"No. But you can have it if you give me back my cape."

Actually, I never did like that cape anyway with all its glittering scales. I thought it was much too showy. So we made the exchange. I picked the cape up from the ground and gave it to him, not too courteously, I am afraid, and he handed me the drum and disappeared into the next arroyo. I was glad about the trade and did not even care that I heard him mutter "dumb broad" as he passed me, and "woman no vagina, woman no heart." The latter was a cruel invective, and no one ever said it to me, although it was true, we ghosts had "no heart," because we were dead. But I considered the source. Quickly I went to fetch my beautiful buffalo skin and spread that out for the birds. Cricket chimed her approval, and to my beating of the drum, we began singing lustily once more:

> Ohey, ohey, ohey yaya
> Bird Spirits about
> We beg for feathers
> Ohey ya.

At the fourth repetition, a glistening, emerald-colored hummingbird swooshed by, twittering in its usual breathless way. "Can't stop," it said, flying by in a deep curve. "Would like to help you out," swoosh, another curve, "but my tail feathers are too small for you anyway." And off it zoomed toward some bright red flowers down in the riverbed.

Crow was the next caller, but he left no feathers either because, as he cawed, he had given a mere two days ago, and there were only so many feathers in one tail.

Then came a pinyon jay, all excuses that he was courting a most attractive young lady and did not want her to think that he was passing through a late molt.

"Do you think these refusals may have something to do with my being, you know, a ghost?" I asked Cricket.

"I don't think so," said Cricket, but by the way she hesitated, that thought apparently had occurred to her also. Maybe Brother Wolf had come to the same conclusion. For a while he had been an interested onlooker, but now he went down into the dry riverbed and did not look back. We found out later that not too far from the red flowers that the hummingbirds liked, Brother Wolf had discovered the lake of Red Water Grandfather in a hidden depression but had had no luck there either. It was Mourning Dove Woman who told us later. "I offered him some of my own feathers," she said, "but he shook his head. They were probably not the right ones."

As far as our own quest for feathers was concerned, Cricket would not give up yet. "There is still a fourth bird to come," she said confidently. "We simply have to wait some more. Everything comes in fours, you know."

But I was getting discouraged and had put the drum down on the buffalo skin when, as Cricket had predicted, a fourth bird actually did arrive. In fact, we heard it before we caught sight of it, the sound a cross between a mutter and a grumble, low in the throat, and then a voice saying, as though the unseen speaker were talking through its nose, "Believe me, really, this hurts me more than it does you, really, but my chicks, they are hungry, really, actually ravenous, really, I am truly sorry, really." And then there it was, a roadrunner, not flying but walking rather fast on

strong long legs, a big bird with rigid, speckled tail feathers, rather short wings, a white belly and small, round white patches under its eyes, and a tousled topnotch as though created in a hurry by an inept beauty parlor operator, carrying a potbellied lizard in its beak. It stepped on the buffalo skin, shook itself, dropped some feathers, and without even a by-your-leave, it ran up the hill behind the house at a healthy clip.

"See," Cricket said triumphantly, "the fourth bird."

But I was puzzled. "Look at the tracks that bird made," I said. "Two toes toward the front, and two toward the back. If I had not seen it arriving, I would not know if it had been coming or going."

"Of course not," Cricket said; "it was a roadrunner. It

has magic, so it keeps its plans a secret. Didn't you know that?" And goaded on by my puzzled expression, she continued, "It's the kind of magic that can make you inaudible or invisible; it can put you to sleep, transport you over long distances; it can bring rain or snow or wind; it can make the melons grow and the corn ripen; it can transform you into anything at all—" As usual, Cricket ran out of breath.

"Roadrunners can do all that?"

"Well, maybe not all of it, but some of it for sure."

I picked up the feathers. "Look, there are three here. We only need two."

"Put the third one in your hair," Cricket laughed. "Ghosts can always use a little magic."

The next morning I painted the prayer stick. With Cricket's help I separated a yucca leaf into strands and tied the feathers to the stick, praying a thank-you to the Mountain Lions as I did so. Then we flew up to their sanctuary and placed the prayer stick next to them in the antler enclosure.

Since we were in the area, Cricket wanted to show me the Obsidian-Covered Mountain, the guardian peak of the west, but we got lost on the way and strayed instead into an enormous, sinister canyon. It had perpendicular walls of slate-gray basalt, dotted sparsely, like a decorator's afterthought, with a few stunted junipers. A wind started up, sighing through the crevasses and agitating the basalt as though its rocky folds were a heavy velvet curtain. As I watched, a huge hand reached out high up on the wall and pushed the tapestry aside, revealing an enormous spectator, his eyes and mouth ringed in black in the manner of the sacred clowns, and wearing a cap with dry corncobs attached to it. I could feel Cricket crawling on my ear lobe. "We have trespassed," she said barely audibly. "That is one of the ancestors watching us. We better get out of here."

I nodded and flew in the direction of what I thought was the exit from the canyon. Instead, its floor seemed to dip even lower, and the sound of the wind was a rolling, mournful moan. Although the light of the sun barely penetrated the shadows, I could see a waterfall cascading down a cleft in the wall facing us. "Look, Cricket, water!" I exclaimed. I flew closer, expecting a fresh spray, but it was not water at all that was coming down but a stream of light. I landed to take a closer look and stepped into what I expected to be a brook. But it was a bed of powdery, gray ashes instead, smelling of fires long extinguished. And the rock-strewn ground around us was barren, not a blade of grass, no rabbit brush, not a sage bush, no plants at all. A big boulder barred the view to the left, and I seemed to hear a voice, so I started walking toward it. And indeed, there was someone on the other side of the brook of ashes and as I went closer, I saw that the singer was a very old woman. She was sitting on a rock close to where the cascade of light was coming down. Her eyes were closed, her deeply wrinkled cheeks were streaked with tears, and her white hair hung in uncombed strands around her face. She wore no jewelry and was dressed only in a black manta that left her emaciated arms uncovered and revealed the top of her shriveled left breast. Rocking up and down as one would in great pain and mourning, she sang:

> Yeah, yeah,
> I am sitting like a weeping willow
> My tears are falling for you
> All my children, your beautiful young bodies
> All my children, your beautiful young bodies.
> Yeah, yeah.

The song was so sad my tears started flowing too, and not wanting to intrude, I flew upward, out of the canyon, to escape the heart-rending plaint. It was a very long way up, but finally I made it to the rim of the canyon. There was a green meadow and sunlight, and I sat down next to a blooming creosote bush, trying to regain my composure.

"I wonder whom that grandmother was mourning?" I finally asked Cricket.

"I have no idea. I have never been here before." Something in Cricket's voice made me suspect that she was not telling the truth, or maybe not the whole truth. "And we can't ask her, so why don't we just leave?"

"Of course we can't ask her. But we can't simply leave. If we knew what this was about, maybe we could console her."

"She can't be consoled."

"How do you know, Cricket? Are you hiding something from me?" Cricket did not answer. "Look, it seems to me that one time when Avanyu, the Rain Serpent, took me with her, I saw a waterfall looking like that. Maybe Grandmother's despair has something to do with that light cascade. We could find out by asking Avanyu to take us there. Let's try, all right?"

Cricket had no objections, although she said that sometimes it was better not to know everything. I stood up, and placing my cupped hands on my hips, I called my rattle.

I felt a sudden weight on my shoulders and then my body began gently swinging sideways. I looked up and saw above me the green and blue zigzag pattern of mighty Avanyu's body. We flew across the land, over giant trees and deer grazing under them; then there was an enormous mountain

range. Lightning flashed across the horizon. We were im-
mersed in fog, then below us there was the round, open
crater of a volcano. I could hear the fire crackling. Flames
shot upward, and it was the tallest, most enormous fire I
had ever seen; but it was not red, it was a grayish blue.
Avanyu must have let go of me because I was now falling
into the crater and indeed, to the left of me, there was what
I had always thought was a waterfall. But when I hit bottom, I realized that it was not water but light; and in a most
singular way, it seemed to be streaming upward instead of
down, carrying with it all manner of debris, trees, flowers,
insects, plants, fish, frogs, even human infants of many
different facial features.

Then I was in a cave, and I heard Grandmother's wailing voice again, reverberating from the walls:

> Yeah, yeah,
> I am sitting like a weeping willow
> My tears are falling for you
> All my children, your beautiful young bodies
> All my children, your beautiful young bodies . . .

The rattle fell silent, and weeping, I collapsed on my knees next to the creosote.

"There is nothing you can do," Cricket said.

"So you have been here before?" I sobbed.

"No, but we all know about Grandmother crying by the cascade of light."

"It is extinction, isn't it?" And when Cricket did not answer, I said, "Let's fly home."

"She won't stop crying," I heard Cricket say. I had tried to stop, crouching by the marigolds, but it seemed that I could not. I kept hearing Grandmother's mournful "my tears are falling for you" over and over again. Then I felt a hand on my shoulder, and when I looked up, it was Buffalo. "Cricket called me," he said and sat down next to me, his arms around his knees.

I felt the comfort of his presence and started calming down. "Where is the stream of light taking all those beautiful children of Earth Mother?" I asked, still choking on my tears.

"Up to the North Star, to the Ancestors."

"Will they ever come back?"

He shook his head. "So there is no hope, is there? More

and more of Earth Mother's children will be carried away, and she will end up weeping alone by the brook of ashes?"

Instead of answering directly, he said, "I was told that Grandfather Diviner wants you to call on him."

"Will you come with me?"

"I will wait for you here."

"Will you then paint me?" He nodded. I lay down, and Buffalo, dipping his index finger into the pot with blue paint that was still sitting there, knelt down and carefully drew a line from below my earlobes and across the bridge of my nose. Then with a thank you I started assuming the posture, repeating to myself as I used to when I was still a human, "Kneel with your left leg, sit on it, right leg up, hands on your knees, head faces right knee, tongue between your lips." The posture had always given me trouble, but I had to admit that as a ghost it was much easier than before.

With the first stroke of the rattle, I found myself in front of the familiar straw-thatched dwelling I had seen so often in my visions, on top of the earth pyramid, where Grandfather liked to stay.

"You have come, my daughter," he said. "I have heard your question. Look."

He pointed to the valley below, where smoke was rising from cooking fires in oval houses. It vanished, and instead I found myself transported once more to that frightening streak of cascading light. Except this time there were many people around, men, women, even children. Some were breaking chunks off the cliffs with their bare hands, and their blood stained the rocks red. Others were loading them in baskets and placing them on their heads; they were taking them to the cascade. There was a slender boy among them, and the basket was apparently too big for him because he was carrying a single rock on his bare shoulder. "Your grandson," I heard Grandfather say, but I could not see his face. At the cascade, still others were constructing a barrier, and as I watched, the ominous stream of light seemed to be getting narrower.

I wanted to see more, but then I was back with Grandfather, sitting with him in front of his dwelling. A boy climbed the stairs and brought a gourd with tortillas and a dish with red chili sauce. "Eat, my daughter," Grandfather said. I took a tortilla, but before dipping it into the sauce, I asked, "Those people who were building the dam, what keeps them going?" "Dreams," he said, "dreams, my daughter. And when you will be a spirit . . ."

The rattle stopped and I was back at the marigolds, and there was Buffalo, nodding to me, and Cricket was chiming in a crack in the old adobe wall. I got out of the posture and sat down next to Buffalo. "You have been comforted?" he asked. And when I nodded, he said with a broad smile, "Although you didn't get to eat that tortilla?"

"So you were there anyway?" He shrugged. "Grandfather insisted."

"I am glad, so I won't have to explain what happened. Say, if I understood Grandfather correctly, I can also bring people dreams about the dam, when I am a spirit."

"Right." Buffalo put his arm around my shoulder. And guessing my thoughts, he added, "Stop worrying. Soon you will also be a spirit."

When later we all sat around the evening's cornmeal, Buffalo and I, Cricket, Brother Wolf, Sister Snake, Old Man

Badger, even the Messenger, whom I had not seen for a while, Buffalo turned to me and out of the blue he asked: "Tell me, why do you really want to go beneath the Lake to stay when you are a spirit? I suspect there is more to it than hearing the cicadas sing and watching the kachinas dance."

It was a beautiful evening. The cloud people had put on a most resplendent show of pink, purple, and golden clouds, and the Full Moon of the Dry Grass had just risen from behind Turtle Mountain. Memories came crowding in, of happiness no longer within reach, of friends not waiting anymore across the road. I looked at Buffalo, and I knew that this was a question I needed to answer for my own sake as well. Why did I really want to stay beneath the Lake?

"I used to have friends at the Pueblo," I started. "They would always invite me to their big fiesta in the summer. You know how that goes: for days on end the women cook quantities of festive food. Relatives and friends arrive from near and far to watch the dances, then they come to eat. You'd be surprised how many come in small groups in the course of that one day, adding up sometimes to as many as five hundred or more. They wait in the living room and visit, then they are invited to sit down to eat. 'Eat good,' the lady of the house says, speaking also to the invisible ancestors that are there, eating along with the guests. Eventually I started helping out, taking fresh food to the table and bringing back empty bowls. Then I also helped wash all those piles of dishes. There I was, standing in the kitchen, washing, wiping, joking with the women. After a while you become part of one body. It is no longer you, it is we. It becomes a dance, a prayer, unimaginably sweet. It must be like that beneath the Lake, I think, not I but we."

Buffalo had listened attentively, and I noticed that the Messenger had also been paying attention, his squash head bobbing up and down. "Right, my girl," he said, "very

eloquently put." And Buffalo remarked, "That is exactly
what it feels like when we buffalo separate from the herd in
the fall and run in small packs." He smiled that broad smile
of his. "Of course we have no dishes to wash, but in that
pack, we are separate and yet part of one body." The
remark stayed with me, but I did not want to seem forward,
so I said nothing.

There were only four more days until the end of my forty
days and I was feeling festive: soon I would be a spirit too.
Buffalo had also stayed longer than usual.

"You know what the Kiowa call this lunar cycle?" It was
obvious he was teasing. "You will like it. It is their Wait
Until I Come Moon."

We, that is Buffalo, Cricket, Brother Wolf, and I, had
crossed the vast valley east of us and were sitting on top of
an ancient, very beautiful kiva, the walls of which had been
worn to gentle softness by the wind. The land was green all
around because this pueblo was close to a river that carried
water year round. Someone was rattling and singing in the
kiva, and the song celebrated the flowers and the brightness
of the morning. Suddenly a heavy gray cloud started ob-
scuring Father Sun's bright face, and at the same time there
was the familiar scraping step of the Messenger audible on
the steps leading up to the roof of the kiva.

"Seed Bearer Woman," he said, and apparently he had
been rehearsing his text on the way, it sounded so formal,
"it now being time soon for you to discard your ghostly
identity and become a true spirit, the Old People residing
beneath the Lake and in charge of the children there have
decided that you still need to go and speak to your mother
in the sacred Realm of the Dead."

I was confused. "When I asked Usa about my mother," I told him, "she said that she did not know where she was. Maybe in another section, she said. How will I find her?"

The Messenger nodded. "Don't worry. She will be there. You do want to see her, right?"

My eyes filled with tears. "Of course I want to see her, my sweet mother."

"You call her your sweet mother?" Buffalo asked.

"In Hungary where I came from, that is what we called the woman who gave birth to us. Our sweet mother."

"Have you seen her after she died?"

"I have on occasion felt her presence, that's all. One time soon after she died, I had a vision where I was in a light blue tower, and there were winding pink steps leading down. I felt that my sweet mother was at the bottom of the blue tower, behind the door. I desperately wanted to see her. So I flew down the steps as fast as I could, but when I got to the door, it was locked. Since then I have tried repeatedly to see her in the Realm of the Dead. As you know, with my rattle I can only get to the edge, and she was not there. But of course I'll try again if the Old People want me to."

Buffalo did not think it would be proper to start my trip to the Realm of the Dead on the roof of someone else's kiva, so he guided us to a valley to the north, round like an amphitheater, shaded by tall cottonwoods and elm trees, and with a fresh brook running through it. I stood with my left arm on my chest above my right arm, closed my eyes and called my patient rattle, "Sound good, little sister, sound sweet."

For a moment it seemed to me as if the rattle were hesitating, then she started up more slowly than usual. I was in a dark tunnel and did not hear her anymore. The tunnel opened up to a foreboding landscape; the air was dank and cold, the earth black. Pale candle flames without

candles flickered under a crooked tree, and on its leafless branches there roosted a group of small, black, hump-backed vultures. "Don't go on, don't go on!" one of them called to me, but I did not stop. A troop of dark riders galloped by to the left of me, and on the right there rose the high walls of a sinister city. A pale light began to dawn, but not on the sky. Instead, the sun was rising below my feet, its light barely struggling through the earth. A swarm of faded violet butterflies arose from a clump of bushes, then I heard voices singing in the distance. I hurried in that direction and came to a river. There was a scent of herbs burning, of laurel and of myrrh, and a voice said, "She should perform her dance for the dead." And another voice answered, "She can't. She is not dead enough. Let her go."

Then I saw her, my sweet mother, whom I had so longed to see again, standing on the bank on the other side of the narrow river. She looked young and well, and all my love and longing for her welled up in me. My father's shadow was behind her, and holding on to her hand there was my younger brother. He had been on his deathbed, an emaciated old man, when I last saw him, but now he was an eight-year-old boy, although looking rather glum.

"My sweet mother!" I called.

"My little one, my angel," my mother answered back. "Finally. Are you coming across?"

"I am only a ghost yet, my sweet mother, I cannot come to you. Why is my younger brother unhappy?"

"He misses you. He wants you to come now. Well, we can wait a little longer. Is it bad to be a ghost? Are you all right?"

"I am very happy. I have all these wonderful friends, Buffalo, Cricket, Grandfather Bear, Grandmother Spider." I could see her shake her head.

"My crazy little girl. Always the animals. But that's all right. You will soon forget them in our beautiful city."

"You are staying in a city?" I tried to hide how appalling that sounded to me.

"Right. You must have seen it coming here. Gorgeous, isn't it"?

I wanted to answer, but I was feeling very strange, getting wispier and wispier. I was about to collapse, shrunk into a heap of nothing, when I felt a presence next to me and two strong hands gathered me up and slipped me into a pouch.

Another moment and I was sitting next to the gaily chattering brook in the amphitheater, leaning against a tree trunk, and Sister Snake was spoon feeding me with blue cornmeal.

"What happened?" I asked, feeling almost too weak to speak.

"Buffalo came to fetch you because you were late returning." Cricket sounded very angry. "We almost lost you! The

Old People should have remembered that those Spirits of the Dead get awfully hungry this time of the year!"

"You mustn't blame the Old People," Buffalo chided her. "Down under the Lake they know nothing of a world in which the Spirits of the Ancestors are not given any food offerings."

"What does that have to do with me?" I asked, beginning to feel stronger with every delicious gulp.

"The Spirits of the Dead that you visited were sucking the energy out of you," Buffalo explained.

I stopped eating. "Oh no, Buffalo, my sweet mother would never do anything to harm me!" I protested.

"That was not her intention. It happens, like water flowing downhill."

"So I will never be able to see my sweet mother again?" I was beginning to feel desolate.

Sister Snake put down her spoon and embraced me. "Of course you can see her again. In a few days, those Spirits will have their own fiesta, their Halloween, when they can go visiting and receive offerings of food. Then your mother will come and visit you."

I turned to Buffalo. "I don't understand why the Old People wanted me to visit the Spirits of the Dead in the first place."

"Don't you see? Soon you will be a ghost no longer and can decide where you want to be."

"You mean I have a choice?" Buffalo nodded. "Well, I can tell you right now that it won't be the city."

Buffalo smiled. "Whoa—all this passion! What was in that mush that Sister Snake fed you? What about the city?"

I looked around the verdant valley. It smelled of moisture and of grass. A deer came to drink at the brook. The air was alive with the song of birds, and a cottontail was hurriedly hopping down the path.

"One of my favorite fantasies as a teenager was a plan where, by some powerful magic, the city would be shrunk and encased in a bubble. It could feed on itself, I used to say." I had to laugh. "I invented recycling much before its time. And I argued passionately that the earth should be left to the animals. It used to upset my sweet mother. She knew little about animals and she loved the city."

I wanted to describe the sinister city to Buffalo that I had seen on my way to the River of the Dead, when we heard someone come crashing through the bushes. Then there was a big splash. Before we realized what was going on, there was Buffalo in the brook, pulling Brother Wolf out of the water. It was not easy, for he was obstinately struggling to free himself of that iron embrace, obviously trying to get back in.

"What was Brother Wolf trying to do?" I asked, but Buffalo did not hear me, flying away with the dripping Wolf in his arms. I postponed my question for when we would be sitting together again in front of Ash Boy's fire, but Buffalo was called away and I sat before the fire alone, pondering the strange events.

After a while, Cricket joined me, crawling into the hairs of the buffalo hide and quietly chiming away.

"Where is Brother Wolf?" I asked.

"Drying out next to the marigolds," Cricket said. "We tried to get him to eat some blue cornmeal, but he refused."

"Do you know what this was all about?"

"Sister Snake says that while you were with the Spirits of the Dead, Brother Wolf discovered the Lake of White Water Grandfather up in the hills. He was sure this time all would be well because it was the fourth lake. But White Water Grandfather refused him too."

"Let me guess: again because he did not have any feathers."

"I am afraid so. Sister Snake says that Brother Wolf threw himself into the brook because he wanted to turn into mist hovering above it."

"And Buffalo would not let him do it. Do you know why?"

"I was sitting in the adobe wall, and I overheard Buffalo tell Brother Wolf that he would have to wait, that something else was still coming."

I spent the next two days trying to comfort Brother Wolf, but it was no use. He lay there by the marigolds, his amber eyes half closed, not eating and hardly moving. A robin came by to cheer him up, then a Rocky Mountain bluebird, a ruby-chested hummingbird, even a surly crow, but it was no use.

It was on the afternoon of the third day when, unexpectedly, the Messenger climbed up from the dry riverbed, just as I was trying for the umpteenth time to coax Brother Wolf to eat something.

"Seed Bearer Woman," the Messenger said, still quite out of breath, "you are to come to the Large Lake. The Wood Spirits want to talk to you. And you are to bring Brother Wolf along too."

"Do you know what they want?"

The Messenger shook his squash head, shiny with perspiration.

"And where is the Large Lake? I have never been able to find it."

"That was because you were not supposed to locate it. Now you are invited. Fly directly north—you'll see it."

I wanted Brother Wolf to hang onto my garment, but he would not do it. So I picked him up, and holding him tight,

I flew north. I flew and flew; it was very far away. Finally, there it was. The Messenger was right. I had been near the Shimmering Mountain before, but I had never seen this island of green that now appeared below. I descended, and there was the Large Lake, embedded in weeping willows and cushions of radiant marigolds.

Shyly, I stepped up to the rim. And there they were, waiting, four Wood Spirits all alike, treading water and wearing featureless brown, round masks.

"Put Brother Wolf down," one of them said, and I was surprised how gentle his voice sounded.

I did as I was told, and there was Brother Wolf, standing very rigidly, apparently expecting the final judgment.

Turning to Brother Wolf, one of the Wood Spirits said, "We can admit you if we like you, but we still find that difficult." And shaking his head, he continued, "You look quite unappealing with that mask stuck on your head."

Brother Wolf stood there, not moving a muscle. After all, what was he to do? Then I heard the voice of Holy Wind: "Use your feather on him!" And suddenly I remembered what Cricket had told me about Roadrunner's magic. "It can change you into whatever you want," she had said. So I pulled the Roadrunner's feather out of my hair, and without a word I stroked Brother Wolf with it along that black line finely penciled between his ears.

What happened next was truly striking. Brother Wolf shuddered, the wolf mask vanished, and in his place there stood a fine young man with long black hair, wearing the embroidered kilt and the strap of cowry shells of the dance. He nodded a brief thank you to me, then shuddered again and turned into a spindle of orange light. The light floated toward the Wood Spirits. They stepped aside, and the orange spindle sank below the water, leaving a faint glow behind.

For a moment there was silence, as though all the grass-hoppers and the mosquitoes, all the mice and all the birds, were aware of the momentous occasion. Then one of the Water Spirits turned in my direction and announced, "Seed Bearer Woman, the Old People decided that you may enter if you wish and stay beneath the Lake."

It was so tempting, the fulfillment of all the wishes that I had harbored at the time I had become a ghost. But that was thirty-nine days ago, and I had learned a great deal since then, about myself, and about this vast, magical reality. My answer was ready.

"Thank you, Wood Spirits," I said, "please tell the Old People that I am grateful for their invitation. Maybe some-day I will come to visit. But in the meantime I will ask Buffalo to allow me to run with his pack."

The Lake sank out of sight and I was standing in the desert, as alone as on that morning when I first arrived. But then the land began to vibrate with that unimaginable power that always announced the arrival of Buffalo, and there he was, holding his drum. He looked at me quizzi-cally, then started to beat out a soft rhythm and began to sing:

> Heya, heya, heya, ho
> Seed Bearer Woman
> On the Buffalo rug
> Heya, heya, heya, ho
> She waits no longer.

There is little to tell about how I finally turned into a Spirit. We flew to my house in the dusk of the day. It was the night of Halloween, and after Father Sun had settled behind the Jemez, the Spirits began arriving. "They are attracted by the marigolds," Cricket explained. They came in small groups, some I recognized, friends, relatives. My mother came with my younger brother and my father, but they were in a hurry, so they did not stay to chat. There were others who were strangers, and some came in huge swarms, like migrating birds in the fall, and you could feel the wind as they passed.

They were all gone when Father Sun awoke behind Stone Man Mountain and started on his daily journey. Buffalo and I were standing on the ridge where I had discarded my human garment. "We will have to leave too," he said. Avanyu, the Rain Serpent, had laid out a thick mantle of fog in the dry river valley. It came rising up almost to the ridge, and as the first rays of the sun hit us, we could see our shadows projected on the fog. And I saw that we were both tall, slender wisps of energy, and we were wearing buffalo horns, both of us, except that next to mine on the left there was Cricket's tiny speck of light.

"I think you have a new name for yourself, right?" Buffalo asked.

"I am now Buffalo Seed Woman," I said.

And then we flew away.

REFERENCES

Behringer, Wolfgang, 1994. *Chonrad Stoeckhlin und die Nachtschar: Eine Geschichte aus der fruehen Neuzeit*. Munich: Piper.

Benedict, Ruth, 1981 (orig. 1931). *Tales of the Cochiti Indians*. Albuquerque: University of New Mexico Press.

Boyd, Maurice, 1993. *Kiowa Voices II*. Fort Worth: Texas Christian University Press.

Chagnon, Napoleon A., 1968, *Yanomamo: The Fierce People*. New York: Holt, Rinehart and Winston.

Cushing, Frank Hamilton, 1979. *Zuni*. Lincoln: University of Nebraska Press.

———, 1986 (orig. 1930). *Zuni Folk Tales*. Tucson: University of Arizona Press.

Fienup-Riordan, Ann, 1994. *Boundaries and Passages: Rule and Ritual in Yup'ik Eskimo Oral Tradition*. Norman: University of Oklahoma Press.

Goodman, Felicitas D., 1990. *Where the Spirits Ride the Wind: Trance Journeys and Other Ecstatic Experiences*. Bloomington: Indiana University Press.

Irwin, Lee, 1994. *The Dream Seekers: Native American Visionary Traditions of the Great Plains*. Norman: University of Oklahoma Press.

McNeley, James Kale, 1981. *Holy Wind in Navajo Philosophy*. Tucson: University of Arizona Press.

Ortiz, Alfonso, 1969. *The Tewa World*. Chicago: University of Chicago Press.

Parsons, Elsie Clew, 1994 (orig. 1926). *Tewa Tales*. Tucson: University of Arizona Press.

Swan, Bryan, 1994. *Coming to the Light*. New York: Random House.

Underhill, Ruth Murry, 1965. *Red Man's Religion*. Chicago: University of Chicago Press.

———, 1976. *Singing for Power: The Song Magic of the Papago Indians of Arizona*. Berkeley: University of California Press.

References

Woiche, Istet, 1992 (orig. 1928). *The History of the Universe as Told by the Achumawi Indians of California.* Tucson: University of Arizona Press.

Zolbrod, Paul G., 1984. *Dine bahane': The Navajo Creation Story.* Albuquerque: University of New Mexico Press.

Felicitas D. Goodman taught linguistics and anthropology at Denison University until her retirement. She is now the director of Cuyamungue Institute. She has authored numerous articles in scientific journals, contributions to anthologies, and seven books, most recently *Ecstasy, Ritual, and Alternate Reality: Religion in a Pluralistic World* and *Where the Spirits Ride the Wind: Spirit Journeys and Ecstatic Experiences.*